The Shallow End

The Shallow End
'A compelling and finely judged novel ...' —*DNA*

'The Shallow End is a little gem of a novel and deserves to be widely read ... An impressively fresh voice in Australian fiction'—The Canberra Times'—*The Canberra Times*

Shortlisted in the Commonwealth Writers Prize 2009 – Best First Book.

Walter
'... retains the reader's attention throughout .... memorable and unexpected'—*Australian Book Review*

Bait and Switch & other stories
'An immensely readable collection'—*DNA*
'Sievwright is a lively writer ... never a dull moment in these stories'—*The Age*

The Shallow End

ASHLEY SIEVWRIGHT

Clouds of Magellan Press | Melbourne

With thanks to Gordon, Nora and Luke

As I was going up the stair
I met a man who wasn't there
He wasn't there again today
I wish, I wish he'd stay away.

1

I was at the Prahran pool. I'd been going there almost every day since I got back from Spain. In Barcelona it was cold and women were wearing fur-collared coats on the beach, but back in Melbourne a hot dry summer was hitting its late December stride. It was perfect weather for hanging out at the pool; lucky really given that swimming laps, working on my tan and being depressed was pretty much all I wanted to do that summer.

I was lying on my stomach with my head turned, absently watching the other people at the pool. This stooge over the other side of the pool was getting changed out of his boardshorts under his towel—you know, like you see surfers do in car parks down at the beach. You don't see it as often at the pool, where there are perfectly good changerooms just metres away. The stooge was, of course, well built in that hulky, too-big kind of way, so this possibly explains his choice of location.

And I swear, he made a three-act friggin play out of changing out of his boardshorts. His struggles with his slipping towel were masterful, teasing his audience with a glimpse of the top of his lily-white ass, but tantalisingly never dropping the towel completely until he finally tossed it aside (ta da!) to reveal he was wearing a pair of shorts not unlike the boardshorts. It was a modern male version of a fan-dance. When he was finished, some wag in the stands applauded. His mate joined in as did a few others who had been watching. One called, 'Brava'.

Before I knew it my black dog had been thrown a bone and I actually laughed. Well, it was only a sharp exhalation through the nose, but it was the closest thing to a laugh I'd managed for a good three weeks and it felt incredible. Sure, I still felt like shit, as if I could cry at the drop of a hat, or more specifically at some soppy ad on tele for health insurance, showing a fetching newborn baby and its mother weeping with joy. Yes, this happened to me—I wept for a whole afternoon after watching this ad. But I was also aware that there was, in fact, another angle on the story. I wasn't OK, but knew I would be again one of these days, and probably soon. With the flick of a switch my old friend perspective, which had deserted me for a while there, was suddenly back at the door looking sheepish for having stayed out on a three day bender. As a result everything seemed so glistening and new, like that slippy newborn baby in the ad.

In that moment of fresh perspective anything seems possible. Of course you realise quickly that 'anything' has never really been possible, and is becoming decreasingly possible as you move through your mid-30s, and of course your life is especially shit at the moment, but for those few moments it feels like being 17 and horny again.

*

I didn't find out until a day or two later, but the same day I had a little trickle of perspective and cracked a smile, at approximately 3.22 pm some guy disappeared from the Prahran pool.

The headline in the newspaper was simply, MISSING SWIMMER. A lap-swimmer had gone missing, had vanished, disappeared. His name was Matt Gray. With a name like that he was asking to disappear really, wasn't he?

Apparently, according to the paper, this guy got to the pool with his mates in the early arvo, lay in the sun for a bit then went off to do some laps. And that was it. He never came back. All his stuff—his backpack and his towel and his wallet and phone and keys—was left with his friends. He walked away from them to do his laps, wearing only his togs and holding his goggles, and he never came back.

I did have a question. Well, apart from the obvious one like, What the hell happened to him? And would everyone be really embarrassed when he walked in and said, Sorry I was just at the market buying some bagels? No the really big question to my mind was, How the hell could they say that he disappeared at 'approximately 3.22'? There is nothing remotely approximate about '3.22'. And somehow that made it so much more pointed and creepy. None of this, Oh, I don't know, he wandered off and we didn't see him around for a while and then, well, there you go, it appears he's missing. No, none of that. It's like at 3.22 precisely he simply went up in a puff of smoke.

I hoped it was just some kind of weird muck-up and that he would turn up all innocent and apologetic and wondering what the fuss was all about.

I also wondered what I was doing at 3.22 pm that day. Whether I was swimming laps, or busy watching that guy do his little fan-dance with his towel.

I came to the conclusion that I was probably just lying there in the sun, feeling the sweat tickle down my ribs, with my eyes closed and my mind satisfyingly blank. Chances are.

*

3

I love the Prahran pool. It's a beautiful relic. It's one of those sixties public swimming pools that are dotted throughout Melbourne's suburbs and are, somehow, as intrinsic a part of their suburbs as the postcode.

The Prahran pool has retained much of its original feel in part due to being adequately maintained enough not to need anything but the most basic repairs over the years. Little injections of botox rather than the full series of disastrous facelifts. It hasn't become one of those big, anonymous, enclosed 'aquatic centres' like a lot of others which all seem very impersonal. No, this one seems like just what it is, a modest little suburban pool in near original condition. In the foyer you can see photos taken on the day the pool opened in the early sixties and there is very little difference to what exists today, except the plants are smaller.

The pool deck is made out of big, square, pebble-mix tiles. The edges of the pool walls are tiled with light blue, ridged tiles, chunky and chipped here and there (chips repaired, I note, with black electrical tape). The pool floor and walls are painted the traditional light blue, but here and there it's either slightly darker or slightly lighter, where slipshod repairs have been undertaken. The men's changerooms are largely made out of chunky moulded concrete, smoothed by 40 years of feet and slippery when wet. The windows of the changerooms are that frosted glass with chicken-wire in them.

The pool is book-ended at the north and south by hi-rise council flats. Built around the same time as the pool these towers are monuments to outmoded ideas of public housing and minimalist building methods. Not only in Prahran, these council flats hover, brown and grim, over some of the most popular and expensive streets in inner-suburban Melbourne. Again, due to being adequately maintained but not in any way refurbished, they too retain, resolutely, a feeling of authenticity. Little boxes built out of what could be exactly the same pebble-mix tiles of the pool deck.

When I visit the Prahran pool I kind of wish I could be amongst women in polka dot bikinis and big sunglasses and men in high-waisted buttoned shorts, or even, if I'm lucky, one of those baby-blue zip-up towelling play-suits that Sean Connery wore poolside in *Goldfinger*. The Prahran pool, on a hot day in midsummer, I feel, should look like that— something really spy-cool from Miami. But of course it doesn't. The architecture and surroundings may be authentic sixties, but too much has changed and the crowd is essentially, disappointingly modern. Not to mention homosexual. As well as being positioned in the middle of the two council hi-rises, the Prahran pool just happens to also be slap bang in the middle of Melbourne's gay ghetto. Down Malvern Road, off the corner of Chapel Street and Commercial Road. Melbourne's G-spot. And on a hot day in the middle of a hot summer you can tell. There are a lot of men preening and posing, but above all perving. It's quite amusing to trace the different kinds of pervs that are going on at any given moment. He's looking at him who's looking at him who's checking him out—it's a veritable cat's cradle of perving.

A couple of summers ago, before I went away to Spain, a friend of mine convinced me to come with him to the pool. It was the first time I'd been and he gave me the low-down on the different areas of the pool with specific regard to homosexual occupation of same. There's a nice big L of lawn curving around the west and south of the pool, a bit browned off due to the water restrictions, with a couple of lonely-looking palms and scraggly shrubs and trees ranged around the edge. The up and down bit of the L on the west

5

side of the pool is the family area, but the base of the L is, so my mate told me, known as the 'Pansy Patch'. Whether just to him or in general I don't know, but sure enough, when I looked down, pansies all in a row. There are bleacher steps all along the east side of the pool, made of concrete and aqua painted boards. The southernmost part of these steps is gay. The northernmost part straight. You don't think there could possibly be such rigid, strictly adhered to guidelines? Go then, and have a look for yourself.

Above the rooms that house sauna, spa and massage room is a sundeck with plastic moulded banana lounges. This my mate called Club Med, but I prefer calling it the Lido Deck. It's a mixed area where the harder of the hardcore tanners seem to congregate, with a bit of sneaky nude-ish sunbathing going on every now and then.

So yeah, perhaps that's another reason I spent so much time at the pool that summer, I admit. Not only did I appreciate this perfect little oasis of sixties kitsch, it was also a great place to do a bit of summer perving on some rather fit homosexual men in a variety of quite revealing swimwear. A single man must take his pleasures where he can.

*

There were a number of regulars I saw at the pool most afternoons. Mobile Mary, a gym-bulked young man who pranced around and around the pool talking on his mobile, or pretending to talk on his mobile. He was very much doing it for attention, though, because I noticed that his phone conversations were louder and funnier when he was parading past some good-looking and appreciative boys (oh how he laughed!) and likewise were pretty much non-existent when he walked past the family section.

Then there were the Rumpelstiltskins. I'd only seen these two a couple of times, but they were a great old couple. They lived over the road in the council flats (they left at the same time as me once and I saw them crossing the road and going home) and they just seemed so magnificently old and wrinkled and slow. He had a bent back, like almost 90 degrees, and she wore horn-rimmed specs with a regal air as if she was maybe a long-lost Russian princess. He would get in the pool in his singlet and just sit there with the water up to his neck. She would swim a few strokes of that old-person breaststroke with her head right out of the water. She would leave her glasses on and her hair didn't even get wet. Then they would get out and go.

Fat Annie. She had really skinny legs but an upper body like a packet of crumpets. She wouldn't give way to swimmers faster than her and would do a tumble turn right on top of you if you happened to be in the way. She gave me the shits and I tried not to swim in the same lane as her.

Then there was Red Trunks. I called him that because, no, wait for it, because he wore red swimming trunks. Is there no limit to my creativity? They seemed a size or two too small for him (gratifyingly), but as he was quite heavily built and big, perhaps that was because he bought them when he was a size or two fitter than he currently was. It was the body that could very soon go either way—either he could regain the structure once again and be hot shit, or he could wake up one day with a white pot-belly. You know? He was very business-like in his swimming. He would get in and do his laps, slow and splashy and plodding, then get out and leave. I developed a soft spot for Red Trunks. He wasn't my usual type, but he was almost the absolute opposite of Spanish Leo and I guess that was the point, right? There had been a glance or two and small nods of recognition pass between us, and given an introduction and an ounce of encouragement, I'd give a fuck a go.

There were others. Not everyone got a name. Not everyone reappeared. Young and old and all shapes and types. With one thing in common amongst the gay boys, dark glasses and baseball caps, eyes hidden but heads alert and scanning, back and forwards back and forwards. Round and round and round. The old cat's cradle of perving.

I felt like these fellow regulars at the pool were friends. They all had their names and some even got a back story. But the truth is, of course, that I didn't know these people. I thought I did, in a way, because I saw them every day, and this familiarity led me to make assumptions about what they were like. But there's nothing to say I was right, or even close. It's funny, feeling like you know people but knowing you don't really. We all do it. People you might see on the tram one morning, or workmates you're not particularly close to but nod at in the lift. Or even people you read about in the paper.

I enjoyed the distance and disconnection of all that pool perving. It suited me that summer. I wasn't engaged with those people, nothing was expected of me. I barely talked to anyone. I'd say, perhaps, a 'hello' to whoever was on the desk when I got there, maybe nod acknowledgement to Red Trunks, but I wasn't quite there. I'd just swim my few laps, dry off in the sun, read the paper, people-watch. Then I'd go home. It was the next step up from wanting to have showers all the time and stay in bed. Sure, while I was out of the house I may still have been wrapped in my 'little cocoon of wallow' (thank you sis) but it was like a scab, where all the healing is going on underneath—you can't pick it off too early, it has to come up from the edges in its own time, bit by bit, with a lovely little itch.

At one point I thought, I wonder if anyone's got a name for me. Perhaps there was a people-watcher watching me, and perhaps he or she had a name for me. And a private story.

Anyhow, my pool routine would end with a tram back into town and another round into the Docklands, where I would buy a six-pack, take the lift up to Sharon's Place and drink enough so that I could sleep through the night.

*

Sharon's Place is where I was staying that summer. It didn't actually belong to someone called Sharon. Nor did it belong to me. I was house-sitting.

My last place in Melbourne was a share house in Brunswick. I wasn't on the lease, and so I could go any time I wanted, and when I did, with only a week notice, they replaced me easily with another renter and so I had nowhere to come back to when Barcelona blew up in my face.

So how did I find myself in a luxurious apartment on the Docklands? The simple truth is that my sister saved my bacon. The truth is often quite lame, I've found. She's in real estate in Sydney, which I can imagine is as fun as going for a paddle in shark-infested waters while someone throws a whole lot of fish guts around you. She's two years older than me, tough as nails but very hard-love-kind, and I adore her. She married a quiet, unassuming kind of guy who is also quite lovely. In their early 30s they decided to start a family but discovered she couldn't have kids and ever since then she's been a fiend for her career.

Anyhow, she apparently knew this fella who was away in the USA and was willing to let me stay there for a bit rent free. He could be back any day, but until then he was happy for me to be there. At least that's what she told me. My sister, needless to say, is a fucking legend.

Sharon's Place is in the Docklands development just west of Melbourne. The Docklands used to be old unused sheds and falling down piers, where I remember going to numerous gay dance parties. Now it's (mostly) colourful apartments and office buildings. The whole of the docklands area feels deserted and unfinished, probably because it is.

It wasn't a bad apartment, I suppose. It was the type with yucca plants and a water feature in the entry hall and a telescope in the living room. All beige and kind of porny, you know? When I walked in my first thought was, *Basic Instinct*, *w* hich is of course why I called it Sharon's Place, which was also kind of handy since my sister made me swear not to tell anyone who the real owner was. (Not that I talked to anyone from one day to the next, other than the skank at the 7-11 who hates my guts ever since the day I knocked her Skittles display on the ground. Accidentally.) All this secrecy was because the owner was *famous*—that is if you give a shit about what he does, which I didn't and don't. Well, I suppose, even if you don't you might know who he is. I did the moment she mentioned him.

My sister would crucify me if she knew I was writing about him here. So from now on I'll just call him X. No. Not X. That's so been done. Y? No. Make it T … That's his initial. That'll do.

Mr T was away from Melbourne a lot and didn't use the place much. It showed. It was totally soulless and barren. Maybe it was all that beige and Smeg appliances. I kind of wished there was some horrible cheese-encrusted waffle maker thing sitting on the kitchen bench, or milk crates as a bookshelf or some really well-worn something or other.

But there were no THINGS anywhere. There were shelves but not things on them.

The whole place, the apartment, plus the Docklands, made me bored and antsy, but at the same time sapped my strength so I could do little but lie around or sleep. There was cable, so there were a million channels but nothing to watch, there was the telescope but I could find nothing to look at. One day I was so bored I just lay on the floor in the middle of the living room. I considered masturbating, but couldn't be bothered and ended up watching flies circling the light-fitting. They circled each other warily, then suddenly one would make a dive for the other and they'd just spin around each other before separating and going back to gently circling again. This dog-fight went on and on and on for however-long before I got bored and went to the pool.

*

In the days following the disappearance there was a lot in the media about Matt Gray.

The first time the disappearance was reported he was nothing much more than a name and a single line of description, 35-year-old Prahran resident. Then there was more to say about him. Bit by bit we found out he worked as an account manager with a local real estate agent, was born and bred in Melbourne's eastern suburbs, and had been a keen swimmer all his life, representing both his school and his university with some success, more recently lap-swimming almost every day to maintain his fitness, but no longer competing. It all made him sound a bit of a yawn.

There were also plenty of details about the day that Matt disappeared, exactly what he said, what he wore, what he did, and when he said and wore and did it. I must admit I scoffed up all these insignificant little details, day after day, like salt and vinegar chips, picking up the crumbs with a licked finger.

On the day of the disappearance Matt's arrival at the Prahran pool was timed at exactly 1.23 pm. He had a membership card, like I did, and the time he scanned through at the front desk was recorded. The attendants on the desk didn't remember him coming in, but the computer recorded it to the minute. Once inside Matt changed into his swimwear, went onto the pool deck and joined a couple of friends, named in the paper 'Paul' and 'Gil', sitting on the aqua steps. He wore green and white striped Speedos, they said, thongs (they think but can't be sure) and was carrying a backpack and a pair of goggles. He joined them for about 30 minutes, lay on his stomach in the sun and did not contribute to the conversation apart from saying 'no thanks' when they asked if he wanted a Diet Coke. Mysterious, hmm? After about a half hour of this, he got up and said it was time to do a few laps. He left his things with his towel laid out on the steps and walked towards the pool. Gil said he watched Matt step onto the edge of the pool and dive into the deep end of the fast lane. Paul wasn't paying particular notice, but he also remembered Matt diving in. There was no fart-arsing around. He didn't go anywhere else, just straight to the edge of the pool where he dived in. And from there, quite simply, he didn't come back.

So where does 3.22 pm come into it? Well, at 3.22 pm precisely (so the call history revealed) Paul received an SMS message from another friend who had finished work early and wanted to see if the boys were at the pool. As Paul's phone beeped and received this SMS message, Gil was looking at the pool and saw a swimmer do a tumble turn, showing a bum clad in green and white striped bathers. This person (Gil was absolutely positive) was Matt.

'It was him,' Gil was quoted as saying in one early interview. It was, apparently, more than just the green and white striped togs. Certainly they were rare and distinctive, but it was more than that, it was everything about this swimmer doing the tumble turn, the skin tone, the hair colour, the sense of the person, the fitness, the tallness. 'I'm positive it was him. Absolutely positive.'

So, doing a tumble turn in the fast lane at precisely 3.22 pm is the last time Matt (if it was indeed him) was officially seen. By his friends at least. There were, of course, many strangers who came forward after the disappearance to say they had noticed Matt that day at the pool. They saw him doing his laps, they said. Diving in the deep end, they said. They remembered him as the one with the green and white striped togs, they said. One unidentified man was quoted without additional comment as saying, 'Oh yeah. I saw him. He was quite nice but not my type.' The timing of these various sightings though was mostly vague, and none of them could be pinpointed as rigidly as Gil's at 3.22 pm, which became the official 'last sighting'.

At closing time, when the crowd dispersed and Matt didn't appear to be anywhere on the premises, his friends Gil and Paul felt there was nothing to do but report it. The police were called. They searched the entire pool grounds and buildings and confirmed that Matt was nowhere to be found. The staff members on the desk that afternoon were interviewed and stated they had not seen anyone matching Matt's description leave the pool through the front entrance, but they were, they said, very busy and could not swear that he hadn't. But of course he must have left. There was no other explanation. Although it seemed highly improbable that he would have done so dressed only in green and white striped Speedos.

Matt's belongings were left on the bleacher steps where his friends had been sitting. His towel, one with thick multicoloured stripes and white fringing at the ends, had remained spread out where he had left it. His backpack was left next to it and contained the rest of his belongings. These included his clothes, underwear, shorts and teeshirt, sunscreen, deodorant, a pair of running shorts and a bottle of water. In a separate zippered section of the backpack was a mobile phone, his watch, his keys and his wallet which contained cash, credit cards, a couple of business cards, an unused Cabcharge voucher, and a public transport ticket. The front pocket also contained his pool membership card as well as a membership card to the Aquatic Centre in Albert Park where he did his laps during winter. So, missing along with Matt were his green and white striped swimwear, his goggles and whatever footwear he had worn to the pool that day.

But what footwear? The two friends said that when Matt emerged from the changerooms and joined them he was wearing thongs. They couldn't be 100% sure but thought they were white plastic thongs. However, as there were no thongs in Matt's backpack, or with the rest of the belongings, or as it turned out left anywhere else around the pool, it was presumed they were missing with Matt. However, while Matt may have worn his thongs out of the changerooms and up onto the bleachers, there was no way he would have then worn them swimming. Which was all well and good, except it meant that the white thongs should have been found with the rest of Matt's belongings, and yet weren't.

I thought to myself at the time, What's with this thong thing? It seemed trivial, but in some way that I didn't have a clue about, those missing thongs seemed especially important. Perhaps it was because they were the only wrinkle in an otherwise ordinary timetable of events? There was no other clue in these chip-crumbs of detail, no indication that something unexpected or extraordinary was about to happen, except for those white thongs, which should have been there but weren't. Otherwise it was just a normal summer day at the pool with fizzy drinks and SMS messages, usual everyday bullshit stuff. No one saw anything amiss or heard anything amiss, and in the middle of it all Matt Gray was just gone.

I don't know what I expected; upheavals, with horses eating human flesh and the earth opening up and a sky full of fire and all that stuff? I don't know. But I suppose you'd like to think that if you were going to just disappear like that there'd be something other than just a pair of white thongs to indicate that something weird had happened.

*

One other thing about all these early articles on the missing swimmer. Many of them were illustrated with the same photograph of Matt. It was a picture that was taken at some work function or other and he looked buttoned up and on his best behaviour, well-built and if not handsome at least regular-featured enough not to be unattractive. He was the type who would certainly have been noticed, especially at the Prahran pool which was, I knew from experience, exactly the place where men noticed other men.

And as I looked at the photo of him, all pixellated the closer I got to it, I became sure that I had also seen him that day at the pool, doing what I couldn't remember, but just like those other strangers at the pool, I too was sure I had seen Matt Gray.

*

15

When I first came back to Melbourne from Spain I got a taxi to the address my sister had given me in the Docklands, to Sharon's Place. I felt like shit, jetlagged and miserable and my stomach and bowels felt horrible.

I got the key from the caretaker's office and went up and went pretty much straight to the bathroom where I shat and showered, then found the bedroom and went to sleep. For the first few days, that's pretty much what I did. I had an amazing appetite for hot showers (even though it was hot) and for sleep. Food I ordered in, or just didn't eat at all. My life, when I thought about it at all during those days, seemed crap, but so solidly and consistently crap that it was, in a way, not as upsetting as it could have been. I mean, when things seem thoroughly bad, they're the times you think, Oh, well, it's not as if I can salvage anything here, and you quite happily have another drink and just wallow in it and, I think the phrase is, 'give up'. That's how I felt. Jetlagged. Numb. Hot showers and sleep and a dumb feeling that it was better not to think about anything was all I could manage.

Anyway, I remember, it must have been three or four days into this, I woke up and had no idea what time it was or what day, or whether it was even day or night. There was, I could see, a bit of light seeping in around the edges of the curtains but it was very dim and dusky. It was obviously, I thought, either sunrise or sunset, but I had no idea which. I went to the bedroom curtains to open them and check where the sun was. The whole sky was this dark brown colour. I could see where the sun was, this washed out, smudgy, round bit of lighter brown almost directly above. It must have been about one o'clock in the afternoon or something, but it was like a total-sky eclipse in brown. I opened the window a notch and you could smell the air, hot and thick with wood smoke. It didn't make a single bit of sense to me until I turned on the news and found out that bushfires had been burning in the east of the state for days. On one hand the browned-out sky was ominous and scary, which seemed perfectly appropriate given my mood at the time and the unholy crappiness of my life, but on the other hand I also didn't give a shit. I just closed the curtains and went back to bed. But you get my point, I think. At least I had the horses eating human flesh, yeah? Matt Gray got a perfect blue sky.

2

In the days immediately following the disappearance I was back at the pool, just as I had been in the days prior to the disappearance. There were a string of hot days just after Matt went missing and so there was a relatively thick smattering of patrons at the pool each day, but one day blended into the next during that time.

The packet-of-crumpets woman was often there. And one day Red Trunks made an appearance. I watched him walk from the changerooms to the end of the pool. His bum was so lovely, each cheek bulging as he walked, left right left right left right. His thighs were big and wobbly, the muscles were there somewhere, but loose like a swimmer's, not tight like a runner or a bike rider or a body builder. I decided I liked his thighs almost as much as his bum.

I lay down on my stomach, turned my head, closed my eyes and listened to the sounds of the Prahran pool. There was the sound of water constantly flowing as the pool spilled over into the filtration system, and splashing of course, but surprisingly the loudest noise was the sound of children screaming. Close your eyes and it's quite disconcerting.

It would soon be New Year's Eve and there were a number of poofs at the pool topping up their tan for the big night out. A little gaggle of them closest to me were talking about what tickets they'd got and whose place they were getting ready at, but amazingly I heard no mention of the missing swimmer. In fact, in those few hot days that melted into each other, everything seemed exactly the same as it had been the day before Matt Gray went missing, which was somehow a bit disappointing and kind of horrible.

The whole thing had grabbed my interest, I admit, but in the way that other summer pastimes do. Like Sudoku or crosswords or books written especially to be read on the beach. Things to pass the time when passing the time is all you have to do.

Lazy and hot, various things about Matt drifted through my mind like they were carried past on a conveyor belt, steadily slipping past the viewfinder before I could properly grasp them or think about them in any detail.

Then sweat dribbled down and tickled my ribs. A sign I was officially too hot to think. Bliss.

*

When I got back to Sharon's Place that day there was a message from my sister on the answering machine. She hoped that everything was OK and that I had to call her. Notice that, I HAD to call her. That was so her. So I called her mobile, hoping for the voicemail, but she answered.

'Hello.'

'I'm just calling you to let you know I'm OK,' I said. 'But I'm not going to talk about anything.'

'Well hello and thank you to you too, you little shit. Are you sure you're OK?'

'Yes I'm sure.'

'You're wallowing. I can tell.'

'Like a pig in shit.'

'OK. Call me again soon.'

You know, I think if you're going to disappear, either from a pool or up your own arse, the time between Christmas and New Year's Eve is the time to do it.

When Ava Gardner came to Melbourne to do that film *On The Beach*, she apparently said something like, 'Melbourne's a great place to do a film about the end of the world.' It's one of those moments in Melbourne's history that everyone knows, like Jean Shrimpton wearing a miniskirt to the Melbourne cup, or Picasso's Weeping Woman turning up in a locker in Spencer Street Station. I think Ava got it right, personally. There's a scene in *On The Beach* where Ava and her co-star, whatever his name is, walk down a Melbourne street and there are empty cars in a motley arrangement all over the streets and there's not a soul around. This is the end of the world as we know it; this is Melbourne between Christmas and New Year. There's little traffic and hardly anyone in the streets. Everyone's either holidaying elsewhere, or staying indoors because it's so hot and everything's closed anyhow.

It's the kind of feeling that can conk you on the back of the head if you're not careful, especially if you don't have family and friends around you to bicker with as a distraction. It's the kind of time when someone who's come back to town with fresh wounds can creep into a stranger's porny apartment to lick them (the wounds not the stranger) without telling anyone he's even there, and who might just possibly, well might just possibly not make it.

Just before I left Barcelona I booked into a ritzy hotel I couldn't afford and proceeded to drink my way through the entire contents of the mini-bar and a bottle of vodka, only stopping when I went to lie down on the bed for a moment, miscalculated and ended up on the floor wedged between the wall and the bedside table where I passed out, only to come to in the freakish dead-time of 3 am in the morning, horribly hung over, and with no more vodka.

I decided that I didn't want to have escaped that Barcelona dead-time (thank God for 24-hour room service and Spanish soap operas) and come so many miles only to get conked by Melbourne's own dead-time. No, what I needed was a night out on the tiles so that at the very least I could get drunk somewhere other than Sharon's Place.

For a split second of madness I was going to call an old friend and long-standing companion of nights-out, Melanie. Possibly the only thing you need to know about Melanie is that she is very loyal and asks few questions, I guess mostly because she wouldn't appreciate any questions about her own lifestyle which I know includes table-top dancing and suspect also includes Centrelink fraud. But even Melanie would require some explanation of what went down in Spain and I just couldn't, so I decided against it.

No, what I needed I felt sure was the comfort of strangers, male strangers, gay male strangers. To make it any more specific might be pushing things.

*

Your everyday workaday gay bars aren't all that different the world over, which I guess is not surprising in that the common denominator is that the patrons are, of course, gay.

Sitges is a little town down the coast from Barcelona. It's a summer resort and attracts all sorts, but it's mainly got the distinct whiff of the international gay tourist. During the summer along the main esplanade the nightlife thumps out of gay bar after gay bar until sun-up. Leo and I headed out one night to taste the delights that Sitges had to offer and found ourselves in one of those clubs. Apart from the fact that there were more Spanish men standing around (which admittedly was a major plus), I could have been at the Xchange Hotel on Commercial Road in Melbourne, just a block or two down from the Prahran pool. The same blacked-out windows to the street, the same bar, pool table, banks of televisions playing film-clips, the same watchful standoffishness of the patrons. They were even playing *Let's Get Loud* by Jennifer Lopez. Or I might be making that bit up. I do know that Kylie made it into the mix.

Even so, the Xchange Hotel seemed particularly uninspiring that night when I got there. I went up to the bar and ordered a drink. I didn't know anyone, but then again I didn't think I would— this wasn't somewhere me or my friends had frequented when I last lived in Melbourne, which that night was just the ticket. I moved away from the bar, found a little ledge to put my beer on and checked out the room. I wasn't the only one doing so. Again, here were people watching people. It was kind of the same as at the pool. And the same as the club in Sitges. Probably it's the same in gay clubs and pools the world over.

All this watching could be either comforting or stifling and that night I felt stifled. I didn't want to stand across the room and look at people and then maybe chat to someone and maybe strike at least a deal if not a genuine connection.

I didn't want to have to bother and so in the end I decided it wasn't too early to go to the sauna. At a sex-on-premises venue there's just as much looking, but not as much standoffishness. And to be honest, I just wanted sex. Not because I was horny, I wasn't particularly, but just because I felt like gorging. I wanted to be a pig and eat with my hands and stuff my cheeks full of sex. I felt lonely. I felt blue. I felt bored with my own company. I also felt, strangely, a little bit scared to stay cooped up in that fugged-up apartment for another night. I know from past experience that these feelings are not erased by piggy sex, but like a sugar pill, it fools you into thinking things are going to be different.

When I got to the sauna, I took off my clothes and put them in the locker, put a towel around my waist and headed through. First thing you see is a row of showers, with usually a couple of men underneath lazily soaping their dicks, strategically placed to see newcomers and at the same time put on a bit of a show if necessary. Then there's a spa with no one in it, a sauna, and out the back, through a pair of saloon-like swing doors, dark passageways and little rooms with glory holes in the walls and packets of lube and condoms left like offerings. In some cubicles there is someone waiting and watching those walking past, or a couple already engaged, or more than a couple.

I kept on walking past door after door, looking in, getting a feel for the place, like some tourist. Stupidly, I was reminded of a cathedral I visited in Spain. It was on a rocky hilltop and to get there you had to walk around and around the hill towards the cathedral and along the way there were little grottos hacked out of the rock and a little white statue of some saint in each one. Every grotto had a different saint, and sometimes there were offerings left there by previous pilgrims, usually ordinary things like strings of plastic flowers or little folds of paper with poems or something. And you'd look for a second, and maybe make the sign of the cross, or leave something. And then you'd walk on until you came across the next grotto. I asked Leo what the different saints were the patrons of, and he could tell me because he'd had a Catholic upbringing and remembered a lot of them. And as he told me I found myself liking the statues based on how interesting I found their calling, but I guess you're allowed to have your favourite saint. Saint James the Great is a patron of Spain and also of rheumatics, which I thought was kind of a weird grouping. Saint Jude is the Patron Saint of Lost Causes which appealed to the skinny-black-pants wearing art student I used to be. But my favourite was Holy Mary of Guadalupe. I can't remember what she was the patron saint of, but it's just such a cool name. So yeah, I was thinking about my favourite saints when I joined a solitary traveller in one of the cubicles, went straight down on my knees and found myself face to face with my first dick in weeks. Hallelujah.

Basically I went for it. And after a while of slopping this guy's dick right into my throat and snorting like a truffle-snuffling pig at his pubes, I pulled my head back, closed my eyes and concentrated on how my lips felt fat and my throat felt stretched. It felt wonderful to have a dick in my gob again, I must admit. But it wasn't enough. Now that I'd got started I had ants in my pants and I wanted one with the lot. I opened my eyes and nosed up this guy's stomach and chest. He turned me around, bit on my shoulders and the back of my neck. Soon enough I felt the nudge of his dick and it was all on. I smiled and closed my eyes.

And so I was fucking again for the first time in, what? Three weeks? Four weeks? Maybe even five? For the first time since, when? Since Leo bent forward in front of me, swayed his back and widened out his stance, opening his hips out like a butterfly to take in every bit of me?

After a while my asshole tingled like my lips and for a moment there was nothing else in my head. At one point I found myself twisting from side to side on the end of this guy's dick, my head back, eyes closed, smiling stupidly, like a blind man swaying to music. I know. Embarrassing.

After I'd showered, collected my clothes from the lockers and was changing, I noticed someone I recognised also changing back into his street clothes. I didn't at first see his face, but I certainly recognised his thighs. It was Red Trunks. He saw me at the same moment I saw him. His eyes widened, then he looked away and his cheeks went steadily and very prettily red. I got a jerk of disappointment that I hadn't found him in a cubicle back there instead of that other guy, which was totally unfair as my guy was hot and definitely a good fuck. But there you go, the grass is always greener.

*

By the way, I remember also that St Anthony is the Patron Saint of Lost Articles and Missing Persons.

*

I don't quite understand why the story of the missing swimmer caught the public's imagination so much, or whether it was the media's imagination and the public just trailed behind obediently. News stories sometimes have a life of their own and it's hard to know why. The story of the swimmer going missing from the public pool seemed just what people needed in that fuck-off dead time between Christmas and New Years Eve. It was mysterious, a mixture of soft and hard news, and somehow a perfect summer story. In short, the story wasn't out of the news for a single day, living on through a press conference with tearful loved ones, a weekend of editorials, letters to the editor and profile pieces.

There was also an incredibly high number of sightings of the missing swimmer. Dozens of them. Not all could possibly have been him, but perhaps one or maybe even two of them were accurate. He was seen walking alone (fully clothed) through the park behind the pool that afternoon (a definite possibility not taking into consideration the fact he left his clothes in the pool with his friends). He was seen on the Malvern Road tram the afternoon after he went missing, looking disoriented and apparently mumbling to himself. He was also seen that afternoon in Chapel Street at a certain restaurant (possibly just an attempt to create advertising for the place). He was seen repeatedly afterwards at various clubs in Melbourne, as well as in Sydney at NYE celebrations, as if he was doing guest appearances like a *Big Brother* housemate or something. He was spotted at the Melbourne airport. At the Brisbane airport. At the Darwin airport. He was seen at St Kilda beach. At Sandringham beach. At the Brighton Sea Baths. At the Fitzroy Pool. At the Footscray Pool. At the

Albert Park Pool. In fact, a number of males of around the right age who made the mistake of purchasing those green and white striped Speedos that summer must have been cursing their choice.

I can't remember exactly when it happened, but one morning, I think it was the morning after I'd been out to blow off a little steam at the sauna, the missing swimmer was finally OUTed. I was wondering when it would come. I mean, it's not that I've got a finely tuned gaydar or anything. I'm usually clueless. But even I was adding up the circumstantial evidence myself during the previous week and coming up with gay gay gay.

Firstly, Matt Gray disappeared from the Prahran pool so right away the odds are up. I wouldn't go so far as to say that this was case closed, but the odds are stacked a bit higher at that location than your usual one in ten. This was even hinted to Mr and Mrs Suburbia with 'I saw him but he's not my type', quoted, remember, without further comment, in one of the first few articles about the missing swimmer.

Then there was the press conference that the family had done a day or two after he went missing. This was the usual deal, with the family pleading with the public at large, and with Matt if he was watching, to come home, be safe, etc, followed by a few questions. The footage was used very briefly on every major news broadcast that day but nothing very extraordinary was revealed, except perhaps for the fact that alongside Matt's tearful Mum, stoic Dad and pretty but conventional looking sister (how Australian it all was) was a man who looked a little like the food guy from *Queer Eye for the Straight Guy*, smartly groomed with rimless glasses. You know the type. This man could have been another member of the family, Matt's brother perhaps, although he didn't look anything like either Matt or the rest of the family. But I didn't think he was another family member. It was something about the way he was referenced by name, Kevin, but never by relationship to the missing swimmer. Talking about the one in ten rule, I bet more than one in ten people watching the press conference asked the question, Who's the guy on the end? But the implications were clear, Kevin was Matt's partner.

Perhaps they didn't know what to call him and so opted for calling him nothing at all. I can kind of understand the thinking behind that, but how horrible to reduce him to some kind of hired-mourner character. Surely if they weren't comfortable with husband or boyfriend, they could have just gone with the non-threatening 'partner' or even, if they wanted to get a bit racy, 'life partner'. Perhaps they didn't want to highlight the fact that Matt was gay and that Kevin was his partner, because it was considered off the point, maybe, not really relevant; or perhaps because it seemed a little too sensational when they were dealing with very upset people. I suppose often the safest option for the media regarding gay relationships seems to be the don't ask, don't tell, no need to mention it mentality.

The point is I was already well and truly there when the headlines trumpeted that the missing swimmer was a poofter. And trumpet they did. What's the point of outing a missing swimmer who has inexplicably caught the attention of the public, unless you can do it like this: GAY SWIMMER STILL MISSING. Pats on the back all round on a job well and subtly done guys. Is the story that he's still missing, or is the story that he's gay? The latter. Obviously. In fact, there was no new news about the disappearance at all. A police spokesperson said a few words along the lines that they were 'following up a number of leads' (unspecified) and appealed for anyone with any information about Matt's disappearance to come forward. That was it. No, the point of the story seemed to be primarily that Matt was gay and that the well-groomed *Queer Eye* looking guy at the press conference was his *partner*. He was finally given that title, officially, in the article.

The interview, such as it was, with Kevin was quite a disappointment. For a start he didn't have anything particularly gay to say, which I'm sure disappointed the journo just as it did the public. In fact, the life that Matt and Kevin appeared to live before Matt's disappearance was hardly a Mardi Gras parade. Don't get me wrong, I know not every gay life is all drag queens and rainbow flags, but that headline, you know, it kind of promised more. At least a glory hole or two.

Kevin came across in the article as a nice, simple, heartbroken man. He was quietly spoken, I presumed, his answers to the questions being considered and short. He was an engineer. He and Matt had been together for 15 years, had met at university, travelled together a little, then returned to Melbourne to 'settle down', mortgaged themselves to the eyeballs in a suburban dream/nightmare in the gay heartland of Prahran.

Matt was, Kevin said, hard-working and 'law-abiding'. Yes, he really said that. So I guess Matt didn't speed or, you know, jaywalk or anything. He was also, Kevin said, generally of a positive and easy-going nature. And of course he loved swimming his laps. He would get home from work, walk through the park at the rear of their property, then zig-zag through another couple of streets to the

Prahran pool. Almost every day he would do his laps and would swim up to 1.5 km a time. He had some mates he used to go swimming with, but mostly just went by himself. It was, Kevin said, a solitary pleasure to him.

In short, all in the garden was lovely, a bit boring, and definitely, somehow disappointingly, not 'gay' in any spectacular way, but lovely nonetheless. In fact, Kevin was photographed for the article in his own front garden and behind him you could actually see a picket fence and a 4WD. The whole picture screamed inner suburb sophisticate at me.

As for the disappearance, Kevin said that he couldn't understand what had happened, but that he didn't believe Matt would voluntarily leave his life and his loved ones, would just walk away like this without word, without explanation. Matt was quite close to his family and especially his sister's kids. Nor did Kevin think Matt could have been overwhelmed or abducted by a third party. He was a fit young man, and alert, and he disappeared from a busy public place in the middle of the afternoon.

So what did Kevin think had happened?

Disappointingly, and quite stupidly I think, Kevin said he thought there must have been an 'accident' or a 'mistake or something'. It seemed a pathetic head-in-the-sand thing to say, but I thought I knew where it came from, and felt sad for him.

In any case, the end result of the article was a lot of not very much. The most important thing that came out was a real sense of Kevin's affection for Matt, and a real sense of quiet, dignified sorrow at his disappearance. Also, the fact that Kevin who was presumably closest to Matt had no idea what had happened to him made the whole disappearance even more mysterious, more final.

Oh, by the way, at the same time as all this, the Prahran pool was also 'outed' as having a 'largely gay clientele', which I thought was hilarious. As well as not being news in any meaning of the word.

*

New Year's Eve I stayed in. Surprise surprise. There were fireworks, two lots actually, one above the Yarra and another right there in the Docklands. It was a bit funny considering the state of the browned-out sky not a week or so before. But the fireworks and the celebrations down below Sharon's Place made my situation feel a whole lot more shitful, in the way that little treats and niceties can make hardship seem harder. I mean, I didn't feel as hopeless as I did in the brown-sky days, and yet perversely I found myself thinking back to those days and how easy they were in hindsight. I lay down but I couldn't go to sleep, I made myself a sandwich but then didn't feel hungry, I ran a bath and couldn't be bothered sitting in it for more than five minutes, and then suddenly the idea of staying inside when everyone else was out with sparklers, drinking champagne and dancing and kissing strangers, began to feel like I'd somewhere, somehow, made a really big mistake. Perhaps it was a good thing, me feeling that there was something going on out there that I was missing out on. I guess in a way it was quite positive.

*

The most interesting aspect of the media 'outing' was that Matt became, in a way, a bit of a poster boy for gay men. It was as if the whole city was in the thrall of the gay-best-friend syndrome. I can see it I suppose. I mean, I never met the man, but Matt Gray on paper was definitely easy to like. He was an Anglo Aussie with a middle-class suburban background, healthy, fit, good (enough) looking, and living something close enough to a typical suburban Australian life that would be familiar to many other Australians, with a partner and a job and a mortgage to chip away at. He would, people might think, be the type to be into sport and barbeques, who would dutifully wash his car and mow the lawns on a weekend, the type who would chat to the neighbours over the fence and bring in their mail while they were away. He would be all these things, but also gay in a non-threatening, non-confrontational, out-of-sight, inside-the-house kind of way. He seemed knowable, like a brother or a mate, he was nice-guy regular, he was palatable, consumable on a broad scale, and he became, as such, some kind of absentee ambassador for gay men.

Joe Public's opinions about Matt in letters to the editor were amazingly positive, even gushing. Some were along the 'I don't like gays, but he seems like a good bloke' kind of track. Editorials on the subject of Matt's sexuality were less gushing but just as positive. A councillor in local government, whose big topic the previous election had been gay marriage and the Government of the day being against it, even went so far as to use Matt and Kevin and their suburban 'marriage' to illustrate his point in the gay media, both in a column he wrote in a fortnightly gay newspaper and on the gay radio station. I didn't hear that last one, but I heard about it and found the transcript online.

Unfortunately, all this guff was horribly off the point. The missing swimmer's absentee ambassador status as gay-poster-boy had absolutely nothing to do with his disappearance or with what efforts were being made to find him. Police reiterated their plea for anyone with any information about Matt to come forward, but these pleas were, sadly, if not drowned out then at least pulled under water now and then by the more abstract ra-ra of the poster-boy stuff. The absence of any real sense of police activity, let alone progress, made it feel very much like there was none. At just over the two week mark people started to suggest knowingly that Matt would never be found, and that his mysterious disappearance would never be solved. I tended to agree with them. It just didn't feel right. It didn't feel like it was voluntary, like he'd engineered his own disappearance to start a new life. It also didn't seem likely that he'd been on the end of some kind of 'foul play'. Heaps of possibilities, but no probabilities.

Actually, with the absence of any publicised activity from the police, the way Matt's loved ones were so ordinary and so baffled, and also I suppose with the objectification of Matt as gay poster boy, the whole thing started to feel, to me anyhow, more abstract. Or do I mean more literal? It felt to me like Matt Gray had quite simply vanished into thin air. Somehow you just felt he was gone for good. That he would never be found. It was terribly sad.
One other thing about all that poster-boy stuff. I knew it wouldn't last. I could smell the backlash like ants smell rain.

*

I was at Priceline buying another vat of Vitamin E cream. Part of my routine when I got home from the pool was to have a shower, smear myself over with Vitamin E cream, then let my skin slowly absorb it while having a beer and a cigga on the balcony. I'm a great believer of toxins-in-toxins-out, a Zen, *Karate Kid* kind of attitude to indulging in the naughtier things in life, like sure you can smoke crack, as long as you eat broccoli and wear 30+.

Anyhow, I was in the line at the checkout and heard these two young fellas in front talking.

'Did you see him on the news this week? He looked nice. He was crying his eyes out at the launch, press conference thing.'

I guessed they were talking about Kevin.

'I don't believe in all this gay poster boy stuff. There's something rotten there somewhere. In fact, I think he did it.'

'Did what?'

'Offed the swimmer guy somehow.'

'He wasn't even there at the pool that day?'

'He could have been.'

'People would have seen him.'

'Maybe he was in disguise.'

'What as?'

'Not as anything. Just in glasses and a hat maybe. Or with his hair parted on a different side?'

'What did he do with the body then?'

'Maybe just left him on the grass with all the people sun baking. One dead body amongst them wouldn't be noticed.'

'But what about closing time? It'd be discovered.'

'I wasn't being serious.'

Then the checkout chick said 'Next please' and they moved up and started their transaction.

One night out of the blue I remembered where I'd seen Matt Gray, and it wasn't at the pool. I think it was that photo of Kevin with the 4WD and the picket fence in the background that made me remember that I met Matt once at a party just before I left for Spain and we talked about a leaf-blower.

It was at Vernon's place, which is a big sprawling house backing onto the Yarra in Hawthorn. It's got huge verandas all round enclosed entirely in fine mosquito mesh stuff and is painted a pale pale faded apricot (amazingly) which doesn't seem to me a colour anyone in their right mind would choose to paint their house.

Perhaps it's an undercoat that was never painted over. It looked like a low-security prison. Melanie christened it the Malaria Ward, which kind of describes it brilliantly. The garden is totally overgrown with quite lush plants (even in this drought—I wonder whether you're allowed to pump water out of the Yarra for your garden?) which effectively hide the fact that there's a large river at the edge of the garden. Vernon loves to tell a story of a guest of his going missing, only to be found three days later floating face-down some odd miles downstream, with his fly open and his dick out, victim of a full bladder and a lurch in the dark.

Anyhow, I remembered, just as I was drifting off to sleep that I'd met Matt on one of those weirdly huge verandas overlooking the Yarra. Everything happened on the verandas at Vernon's house. There were a few men standing there looking out at the bend in the Yarra through the overgrown garden. They all held beers and stood around in that slightly formal half-circle that forms at

Australian parties when there is a view, a game to watch, or a BBQ to stare at. Matt was one of the semicircle. Taller than me. Heavily built with a square jaw, squinty eyes and thick features. A real Anglo-Aussie type. That night he was all fresh-shaven, damp-haired and pink-ear clean. Not a dog, but attractive because of his size and fitness rather than his face.

And he was talking about a leaf-blower. It was autumn. There were shitloads of leaves around everywhere. In gardens and gutters. He had just purchased a leaf-blower and was telling the group about what it did and how he'd got a good deal on it. I of course didn't give a flying fuck about his leaf-blower, but I said, 'Oh yes', or something else non-committal and a little dismissive and I'm sure, I'm absolutely positive, that he threw me a look then. Although what that look meant I can't quite remember. I must have had an impression at the time, if I bothered to think about it, but I don't remember now.

His companions in that semicircle were 'his kind of people' with ironed chinos and crisp checked shirts. All holding a beer. Some, most, were a little older, but they were all of a type. I imagine they all had property, with gardens, some maybe even pools, and probably all with leaves. Some had wives. Vernon had a thing for straight and usually married men. Matt, as we now know had a 'husband' in Kevin. It was one of those comfortable but fairly limited home-ownership types of conversations—the type in which I am never much involved or interested, unlike Matt who seemed to fit in OK.

But that look, that fleeting little look. What was that all about? I closed my eyes and tried to call up the memory. I could see it fine. It was an amused, self-deprecating, eyebrow-raising kind of look that said something like, 'Boring I know.' And maybe, 'Aren't we funny?'

I nodded and smiled at him, then went in search of Vernon and Melanie. I didn't, I don't think anyway, see Matt again that night at Vernon's. It was a sprawling party and I had arrived late.

How much of my memory of that small interaction with Matt back then is real and how much of it isn't? How much do we touch-up our memories? Give them a careful brush with turps to bring up the colour a bit clearer, or airbrush them, tuck in the edges? Especially when we remember, or tell ourselves we remember, something that happened on the hop, in the peripheral, without at the time having taken a moment to stop and stand still and make a concerted effort to commit it to memory.

And now of course, writing this, I'm trying to remember what it actually was that I first remembered months ago. So my memory is two or three times removed from that moment at Vernon's place and only getting further removed each time I think about it. No matter what I do, no matter how hard I try, it's like I'm reciting my 7x table or something and the distance between the moment I spoke to the missing swimmer and a reliable memory of that moment multiplies.

3

Now, I like a nice golden glow as much as the next man, but I didn't want to end up as brown as Bastey Boy. He was at the pool almost every day that summer, and every day he lay in the exact same position on the grass in the pansy patch, oiled himself up and cooked himself in the sun. He was the most disturbing colour, I think because it was literally brown. Not the nice light golden colour that I think of as like the little peaks of a shepherds pie when it comes out of the oven, but literally brown. Can I say it again, Brown? It's not a really nice colour for your skin. Seventies furniture yes, skin no. He was a hard one to name actually. There were a few possibilities. He walked kind of like a ballet dancer (feet pointing out) looked a little bit like he was maybe in a Duran Duran cover band (white blond fluffy hair), so it was either gunna be Rudolph or Duran but Bastey Boy stuck so Bastey it is.

So the point is, yeah, I decided to have a day out of the sun and had re-settled myself in the shade this day when Red Trunks showed up and saw me. I mean, let's be honest, I knew, you knew, we all knew this was going to happen the moment I saw him at the sauna, right? I just looked up from Bastey and there was Red Trunks, standing near the exit of the changerooms looking straight at me.

I did that chin-raising backwards-nod hello thing that you do when you kind of don't really know someone to talk to but want to acknowledge them.

He stumped directly up the steps towards me, not particularly graciously or anything. His face was stern with a kind of studied disinterest.

'You're in the shade today,' he said. I'd never heard his voice before and it was deep, serious and slightly off somehow. Maybe his 'r's had a little bit of 'w' in them or something like that? Whatever it was, and it was only subtle, it was hot. I'm a bit of a kink about speech impediments.

I answered him. Almost. I mean, you have to understand this was actually a red-letter day for me. It felt momentous. Like it was the first time I'd spoken to someone since I returned from Spain. Of course it wasn't. I mean, I'd spoken to my sister a couple of times and to people who served me at the 7-11 or the IGA. Or people on the desk there at the pool. OK, lots of people, but it felt different. It was face to face and it was social. My throat felt closed up and when I tried to speak it came out all funny sounding and full of phlegm, so I cleared my throat with a little 'huh-hmm' and tried again.

'I'm having a day off,' I said. It came out that time.

Without asking if he could, he set his towel up on the step next to mine, during which I was rewarded with a nice close-up of his ass. However, even given his ass and his speech impediment, I have to admit I didn't really want him to sit down next to me. It felt awkward. It felt unwanted. Now, here at the pool, where we might have to talk. I mean, it would have been different having sex with him in the sauna. Anonymous, wordless sex was a hundred times easier than awkward conversation. And I felt instinctively that this would be awkward. He seemed like the stolid non-chatty type, and I was all raw and withdrawn. I just wanted to be alone and wallow until the scab had hardened. But it turned out fine. He didn't talk much and neither did I. We just sat there side by side, watching what was going on which wasn't much of anything really. Bastey Boy basted. The packet of crumpets turned up and hogged the medium lane in her usual style. Otherwise, the cute boys were a bit thin on the ground so there wasn't much to observe in that direction. It wasn't all that hot and it was a weekday. But I liked these mild days, when it was warm without being too hot. Not too crowded. A little plane flying overhead every now and then. Red Trunks and I just sat there in silence, and what could have been tense and, you know, an effort, actually began to feel easy and nice. Nicer than a conversation, any kind of conversation, would have been.

After some time he said he was going to go and do his laps. He got some 30+ out of his bag which he quickly and efficiently rubbed into his legs and chest and arms. He then asked in an offhand manner if I could put some on his back. I said of course I would and he sat on the step directly in front of me. His back was broad and meaty, the muscles there, but not well defined. His body was chunky and pale and big. Big shoulders, big thighs, big ass. His skin was pasty white and, up closer, I could see was chock-full of freckles, although these were also pale. Without the 30+, I guessed he would end up one big freckle. I rubbed the lotion in conscientiously and Red Trunks moved a little under my hands, stretching or flexing whatever area I was rubbing, leaning forward and with his arms just a little out. It was a subtle but intimate moment. It felt so good I wanted to put one of my fingers up his bum then and there.

Before I could (as if I would have) he thanked me, picked up his goggles and went off down the aqua steps towards the pool. He looked back at me out of the corner of his eyes, with his head slightly down. He was blushing. So he knew exactly what he was doing. Of course he did. He wanted to get some physical contact under our belt.

As I watched him go off towards the other end of the pool, I thought of course about Matt Gray stepping off towards the pool to do his laps and never returning. And I wondered suddenly, Did I see him that day or not? That day, for some reason, I thought I probably didn't, but that if you gave me enough exact times and details, gave me enough photographs, they'd be like glue and scraps of paper and I could make you a papier mache balloon shape that would be there long after the balloon has deflated. I was just like the rest of the public who thought they 'knew' Matt, or at least someone just like him, just like the rest of the people there at the pool that day who convinced ourselves we had seen Matt just before his disappearance. But none of us could tell anyone anything definite, anything definitely useful. For all the people looking, none of us had seen anything at all.

When I came out of my little zone-out, I looked for Red Trunks but couldn't find him. It freaked me out for a moment. I thought, Shit, surely it's not happening again. What is this? But of course it wasn't happening again. There he was, already in the water, adjusting his goggles. Then a few steps down the lane and a dive into the water and up into a lazy freestyle. I kept my eye on him for a while, thinking of the contact between my hands and his back and feeling horny.

There's no need to draw it out. The short version is that I took Red Trunks back to Sharon's Place on the tram. I didn't actually ask him back and he didn't actually ask if he could come, but when he got back from his laps, towelled off and began packing up his gear I packed up mine also; when I got on the tram he got on too. We sat with our thighs touching and I felt air-headed, as if I wasn't noticing a thing around me, yet at the same time fiercely concentrated on him and the sensation of my thigh against his thigh, and the precise distance between our hands, or our feet.

When we got in the lift back at my building at the Docklands, some old bird popped in there with us. We remained completely silent as we pushed our respective floor buttons, but the old bird who looked like Betty White from *The Golden Girls* acknowledged me with a smile. I smiled back although I couldn't remember having seen her in the building before. She got out a few floors below mine and as soon as the doors began closing I raised my eyebrows at Red Trunks in a meaningless way and made a kind of 'get her' kind of face. Red Trunks gave a little nose-breath of laughter. It meant nothing, but keeping quiet had by now stretched on for so long there was nothing left to do but to make fun of it and make it into some game. Red Trunks picked up on this and played along with several of his own small non-verbal communications, like gesturing with his hand for me to exit the lift first when the doors opened. I did an exaggerated head-incline of thanks as I passed him. It was all really silly, I know, very childish, but it felt wonderful to be feeling seriously horny and at the same time really silly and frisky with it. I felt like Red Trunks and I were going to go off like rockets.

Sure enough, as soon as the door closed behind us in the foyer of Sharon's Place, we were at it. We kissed and groped our way between the doorstep and the living room. There, having very definitely been given the green light, there was just one thing I wanted to do now I had Red Trunks in Sharon's Place. I stepped behind him and dropped down to my knees, pulling down his shorts and underwear with me to reveal that chunky, boxy, white bum. I then buried my face between his cheeks, nosed right in nice and deep and took a big yoga-like breath. He smelt of chlorine, perspiration, and deeper down there the subtle, slightly stale smell of his asshole. It was incredibly beautiful.

After a bit more groping and kissing and undressing I broke the silence by asking if he'd put his red trunks on. He frowned for a bit in thought, then broke his own silence with, 'But they're damp.'

He was only teasing.

×

I have no idea what time it was when he woke me up and said he had to go to work. We'd had sex a few times and slept and ate in between. He said that he would come back after work and how would he get in? I said sure sure, that he could just buzz and I'd let him in. Then I went back to sleep.

When the buzzer went at 4 am I was all hot and groggy and disoriented. I buzzed him in, left the door open and went back to bed. I heard the lift ding open in the distance and a little later the front door close. Then nothing until I felt his presence in the room. He sat on the bed, lay messily across me and kissed the side of my head. His clothes and hair smelt of cooking smells and his breath, just, of whisky and peppermint.

'Wake up,' he said.

I couldn't quite decide yet whether he was arrogant or just simple, but I didn't mind a little bit of either. He woke me up sufficiently to have sex again and then we went to sleep. The next morning I woke early, not being used to someone in bed with me, and instantly wanted to get up and out. I've never been very good with the morning after. Who is?

I called my sister again. If I didn't do it regularly she was quite capable of mobilising some kind of intervention team to infiltrate Sharon's Place to drag me away to be institutionalised. This time our conversation went,

'I'm still OK.'

'Good. And still wallowing?'

I told her I was. Then I asked her if it was true what they say about Mr T, that he's a big old closet case.

'Oh that!' she said dismissively.

'Well you met him. Was he at all swishy?'

'No he was not. He was quite masculine and lovely.'

'A-HA!' I said.

'You're obviously on the mend. Why do you ask?'

'Just this place. It's got a vibe.'

She said, 'OK, yeah, sure.' Then made me promise to call her soon and we hung up.

I went and checked the bedroom. Red Trunks was still fast asleep. His real name, by the way, was Rusty, believe it or not. His brother was called Bo. Bo and Rusty Gilbert. Not Beauregard and Russell, but literally on the birth certificate, Bo and Rusty. I asked if his parents were American. He said, no, just a bit fucked up. He said he was never ever actually called Rusty, and made me promise never to call him that. I crossed my heart and hoped to die, but of course I fully intended to drag it out every now and then, when the opportunity arose. I said I'd been calling him Red Trunks in my head for weeks and would just go on calling him that. Or RT for short.

I went for a walk around the Docklands, then went to the IGA for the papers and back upstairs. In the lift I noticed the headline was again about the missing swimmer. It said, MISSING SWIMMER—WHO IS THE BLOND? I scanned the page

For a start wasn't there a typo there? Didn't blond have an 'e'? Or maybe not? I'd read somewhere that it was 'blonde' for women and 'blond' for men, one of the few times in English that there was a masculine and a feminine spelling for a word.

There was a new picture of Matt Gray on the front page and after a bit of looking at it I realised it was, somehow, the perfect illustration of the missing swimmer and his story. The journalists were obviously digging up more pictures of him as the days went by. At first there had only been the one picture, repeated a couple of times, the one of Matt Gray at some work function looking stiff and formal, but every feature clear. Since then there had been other pictures dug up and used to illustrate the various stories, presumably from family photo albums. There had been the one of Matt smiling, next to his partner Kevin, obviously at some backyard BBQ or something, a Hills hoist in the background. Another of him on a holiday somewhere, wearing sunglasses with only blue sky around him. But now it seemed that they had hit paydirt. Somewhere, somehow, they had found a photograph of Matt actually at a swimming pool, although whether it was the Prahran pool or not it was impossible to tell. There he was, standing in his speedos on the pool deck, fit and happy with goggles around his neck, and water still beaded on his skin, his hair wet and sticking up in peaks, smiling broadly at the camera. He had obviously been standing with other men who had been cropped out of the photo for publication as his arms were held away from his body, as if across other people's shoulders, and one of these unseen people had their arm at his back. It must have been part of a photo of some swim-team or squad, probably if the smile was anything to go by at a time when they'd won something or been successful in some way, even if there was no evidence of a medal or anything. Here was a young Australian man, happy and healthy, celebrating some sporting success with team-mates, the sun was shining, he was at a pool somewhere. There was even something about the brief togs and the contact of male arms on male shoulders that hinted at the gay background to the story. But it was something about the way the face was blank with pleasure of the moment which foreshadowed his disappearance and made it heart-breaking. It wasn't the clearest photo of Matt Gray in terms of features, he was squinting and the sun somehow managed to flatten his features and made his teeth one long band of white, as if he was wearing a mouth-guard, but in another way it was the perfect illustration not of Matt Gray but of what he had become. It was a picture of a missing swimmer, not a man. And the moment I looked at it, I knew that every young man's sister, every mother, every brother, every mate that saw that photo would think they understood something of this person and something of the emptiness and sadness that his own intimates would be feeling.

I only had time to get the gist of the story, being that the police had finally managed to interview an employee of the centre, who had been on duty during the afternoon of Matt's disappearance and had seen him at the pool with an unidentified blond man.

Before I got any further, Betty White got in the lift at the gym level. She had a pale tracksuit on and a white towel around her neck. Her white hair was perfectly coiffed into a helmet, but a little wet with perspiration around her brow. She looked like a *Star Wars* stormtrooper who'd just been on the treadmill. Her eyes went from me to the headline on the paper I had open across my arm.

'Now this is a mystery?' She tapped the paper and clicked her tongue. It was strange to hear her speak with an Australian accent when I expected an American sitcom one.

'It's horrible,' I said, then for some reason added, 'I knew him.' I instantly wished I hadn't said it.

'Oh did you?' Her expression was a mixture of extreme concern and ghoulish excitement. 'Oh you poor thing.'

I blushed and felt like a fake.

'It must be so hard,' she continued. 'Not to have any idea?' She gave me a gimlet-eyed stare of interrogation.

I said that, actually, I didn't know him very well and had no idea what had happened. I wished she'd just fuck off now.

'Oh,' she said, back to normal. She considered me for a moment, then, with a glance at the lift number she said, 'Tell me, is it true what they say?'

I asked what, in particular, she was referring to.

'That he's Jewish?'

I laughed. She looked first shocked then conspiratorial. The lift stopped and she stepped out, giving me an 'oh stop it' kind of look and a light tap on the arm on her way out.

When I got upstairs, Red Trunks was still in bed and asleep. I looked at him for a second from the doorway. He slept quite handsomely, of course, but I found I couldn't quite drum up that little thrill you get when you first see someone new asleep in your bed, because it wasn't really my bed it was Mr T's and the whole thing looked like something that had nothing to do with me, like I'd come into the wrong hotel room or something. And anyway that room, it was all so beige.

I went out to the kitchen and made myself my usual brekky of Fruit Loops and coffee, then went out and ate it on the balcony. I spread the newspaper out beside my plate and read the latest developments on the missing swimmer.

It turned out that after his shift that afternoon one of the lifeguards from the pool was off on annual leave and was heading over to visit with his mother and younger sister in the Coorong where they would fish and dig up pippins out of the sand and live in a little shack and caravan set up for a few weeks. This back-to-nature retreat of his meant that he wasn't reading newspapers or watching television and so didn't hear that Matt Gray had disappeared from the Prahran pool on his last day of work before holidays.

The whole back-to-nature drop-out thing seemed slightly incongruous to me, but then again who could make up that bit about digging pippins out of the sand if it wasn't true? And what was a pippin anyhow? Some kind of mussel? It didn't seem particularly in character, but then again I didn't even know which lifeguard it was.

Anyhow, finally this guy returned to civilisation and got the messages on his answering machine, realised that someone had gone missing from the pool and that the police were desirous of an interview with him. So he called them. And soon the journalists called him.

He knew Matt by sight as he was a fairly regular attendee at the pool, but didn't know his name and had never spoken to him other than general greetings. Yes, he had seen Matt at the pool that day and seen him cross from the bleachers and enter the pool to do his laps. Yes, he was wearing his green and white striped togs. This would have been 2.00 pm. He remembers because he was watching the clock that day, keen to get off.

A little after that, say at about 2.20 he noticed Matt standing at the shallow end of the pool, resting it seemed, talking to a blond man standing beside him. It seemed, he said, more like a casual conversation than one between friends. He got the impression they had not met before, or possibly only knew each other as acquaintances.

The man was of mid-height, stocky, with dirty-blond hair and had a very slight accent that he couldn't identify. Perhaps Polish? Something European.

Taken through the photographs on the Prahran pool database, he didn't find a photograph that he could identify as the blond man Matt was seen speaking to, so he wasn't a member of the pool as Matt was.

After this, the police revisited one of the witness statements from earlier on and saw that one woman said she had seen Matt talking with a man at the end of the lap pool that day who matched the description of the blond man. She had no idea what the time was, but with the lifeguard's more accurate information it now became clear that the blond man was the last person known to have spoken to Matt.

So, the only sighting after this was Matt's friend Gil's apparent sighting of Matt doing a tumble turn at 3.22. But that, remember, was in no way a confirmed sighting, being basically only of a swimmer in the right type of Speedos doing a tumble turn at the deep end of the pool.

Red Trunks was moving around inside, getting something from the fridge, his feet slapping on the kitchen floor. I felt myself go a bit stiff and morning-after weird, but when he shuffled out onto the balcony, looking messy-headed and sleepy, he put his hand on the back of my neck and read over my shoulder for a few seconds, and it felt all un-stiff and fine and my shoulders relaxed instantly. Nice.

'What's this?' he asked. 'A blond man?'

I told him briefly the story.

Red Trunks listened for a moment, then reached down past me and tapped the picture of Matt Gray standing grinning poolside.

'That's me,' he said.

There were a few minutes of confusion before I realised he was actually pointing to the disembodied arm in the photo, the one around Matt Gray's back, the arm of the person who had been cropped out of that photo.

Like a roulette wheel my head spun around and the ball jumped a few slots and clicked in place. Red Trunks had been there with Matt. On that team. In that picture. In a rush, I remembered then that RT had told me his surname was Gilbert. Gil.

I asked Red Trunks if he was 'Gil' from the newspaper stories about the missing swimmer, and he said, Yep. Just like that. Then he said he needed to have a shower and disappeared inside.

Red Trunks is Gil, I thought to myself. Then again, Red Trunks is Gil. It felt like a scoop somehow. Like I had discovered something amazing. I felt I had to act on this knowledge, or ask some canny question of him or at the very least report my findings to the police and possibly offer to keep him in the apartment until they arrived. I felt like my name was on the VIP list at some fabulously exclusive club, you know? And with great power comes great responsibility. Then I calmed down a bit and realised this was no big deal. So I'd ended up hooking up with someone who knew the missing swimmer. It wasn't such a coincidence, especially given the common denominator of the Prahran pool.

The whole thing made me feel even closer to the mystery of Matt Gray. I looked at the photo on the front of the paper again, at the missing swimmer's grinning sun-flattened face and squinting eyes and at the arm at his back that turned out to belong to Gil, who turned out to be Red Trunks.

I wondered for a second how RT felt being cropped out of his fifteen minutes of fame, but then I thought that was a trashy thought and vowed not to say anything about it to him when he came out of the shower for fear of being seen as entirely thoughtless. But I wasn't sure I'd be able to stop myself. I wanted to know about Matt and about that day at the pool and about everything. I wanted to know things that weren't in the newspapers. I wanted the VIP treatment. The unauthorised version.

When Red Trunks came out of the shower, all wet hair and red nose, I had composed myself a little and managed to behave relatively normally. When he'd made himself some toast he came out on the balcony to eat it and read the same article I had.

'So you knew Matt?' I said nonchalantly after some minutes, which I'd counted down second by second.

'Yep,' he said.

'And this blond guy?'

He shrugged his shoulders and said he had no idea. He had already turned the page and was reading another article.

I was beginning to realise that with Red Trunks this whole strong and silent thing which I had thought was just a nice uncomplicated-sex kind of game was actually as ingrained in him as the grain in teak or some other stiff, non-speaking, fucking-annoying hardwood.

That afternoon RT and I were back in bed. We'd been out for a walk and stopped off for a big pub lunch in South Melbourne. When we got home we closed up the curtains to cut out all but the smallest glow of daylight, had more silent sex and following that a post-big-lunch, post-couple-of-beers, post-sex sleep that was deep and long.

When I woke up my nose was in his neck and my hand across his chest. It was hot in the bedroom and there was a sticky but not unpleasant heat between us.

'Will you tell me about Matt?' I asked him.

He made a snuffling noise then said something like, Huh?

'Tell me about Matt Gray.'

He didn't move on the bed, but asked more distinctly this time, 'Why? What for?'

'I mean, if it upsets you to talk about it or think about him, then I don't want ...'

'It doesn't upset me.'

Then he moved his shoulder and said, 'It just seems ... pervy.'

Pervy? OK. I chewed over that one.

Then I told him the story about the woman in the elevator that morning who'd asked if Matt Gray was Jewish. I told him to show him that, well that everyone was interested in knowing about the missing swimmer and that his story and the details of his life kind of belonged to everyone now. But I didn't think Red Trunks would appreciate that point of view. I doubt anyone who really knew Matt would appreciate that point of view. I think it's valid though.

Straight after the elevator story and in the middle of these thoughts Red Trunks said,

'I don't know what happened to him,' in an end-of-story kind of tone.

Then he rolled over more completely away from me and I was presented with his big pale-freckled back.

4

The week after that was pretty much filled with three things, sex, sex and sex. Red Trunks became a regular fixture at Sharon's Place. He didn't move in, but he didn't go home much either, if you know what I mean? He just kept coming back.

He worked as a waiter in the city at a club that was new since I last lived in Melbourne. It was right on Swanston Street near the Town Hall, three stories up with a big bar balcony overlooking the street, a dining room inside and above that a band room as well. It reminded me of the Supper Club, or the Gin Palace or something like that, all fleur-de-lys and gilt frames, tatty decadence. It was the sort of place where Red Trunks was expected to light people's cigarettes for them. I went there with him at the start of one of his shifts one time to have a look. When we got there he went into the bathroom with a comb and came out with his hair parted down one side and slicked down, with visible comb lines in it. Of course he looked gorgeous. I put an unlit cigarette between my lips and he told me to fuck off.

He had a roster that gave him a Monday/Tuesday weekend and threw in a Wednesday every second week for a bonus long weekend every fortnight. He didn't start until 7 pm and worked through until the early hours of the morning. He then came back to Sharon's Place, usually woke me up for sex that was all sleepy (me) bone tired (him) or pissed (both of us), then he would sleep until about midday the next day.

We'd go out for a late lunch, then go to the pool and I would tan while he did laps. It was funny to be there at the site of so many Red Trunk pervings and to have Red Trunks sitting right there beside me. Then we'd come back to Sharon's Place, I'd do the Vitamin E thing, we'd have something to eat and maybe have a few beers and watch some tele.

In short RT slipped sideways into my summer routine without a wrinkle. He was easy to get on with. He didn't talk much and he didn't ask questions. I told him I'd just come back from Spain and was finding my feet again and didn't really want to talk about it. He just nodded and never mentioned it again. He was apparently in a bit of a summer limbo himself, having recently graduated in a field he was no longer interested in working in. In the end we agreed to respect each other's limbo status, spit in our palms, shook hands and pretty much just had sex a lot. Pigged out on it actually.

The only fly in the Oil of Olay was that RT got a bit prickly if I asked about the missing swimmer, so very soon I stopped asking. Well not as often. Don't get me wrong, on one hand I felt comfortable with how quiet and self-sufficient RT was proving to be. It was the perfect level of non-involvement for me in my frame of mind at the time. But on the other hand I felt cheated, like I'd hooked up with an oracle only to find he had laryngitis.

Then there was the stench of backlash. Remember that? Well, over that first week of being a sex-hog with RT it came, slowly at first, but like a mobile phone ring tone it got louder and louder until you had to answer it. The tide of public opinion, along with the media, that little slut, gradually but surely began to turn on the missing swimmer.

The whole thing reminded me of a story I read once about the Renaissance, or some time like that. Apparently back then it was fashionable for young virginal ladies to keep ermine as pets, those little ferret-like guys with fur as white as snow. They used to carry them around in little baskets, like Paris Hilton carries a lap-dog in her handbag. It was considered cutesy. They would have their portrait painted, with their boobs, you know, pushed up, and their eyes all knowing and slutty, and their ferrety snow-white ermine on their lap as a sign of their purity. Anyhow, it was believed that if the fur of these snow-white ermine ever began to discolour it meant that the young lady was no longer a virgin. I thought about this story, (which I don't know if I've got right now, so don't quote me on it) because if the missing swimmer had been a Renaissance virgin, his ermine would have been looking kind of spotty around then.

The backlash started with an article which reported that Kevin and Matt had in fact actually separated at the beginning of December after a long time of estrangement within the relationship and that Matt had, in fact, only a week and a half before his disappearance moved out of their house in Prahran into a one-bedroom flat a couple of suburbs away in Hawthorn.

This was quite a surprise given that Kevin's initial despair had been so thoroughly believable. But then again, as I'd heard first hand in Priceline that day, maybe not everybody believed in the rosy, poster-boy relationship, even back then. I guess they were right and I was a gullible chump.

Kevin went on to explain that he honestly loved Matt and believed that this separation was just a 'break' and that they were going through one of those rough patches that many others couples went through.

When asked why he had lied earlier, or at the very least misrepresented their relationship and withheld the information that Matt no longer even lived with him in the terrace in Prahran, he said that he did not feel he had lied or misrepresented the situation at all.

'Taken all in all,' he was quoted as saying, 'we've been together twelve years and apart two or three weeks. Which one would you say properly represents our relationship?'

Kevin reiterated that he didn't know what had happened to Matt, but that he didn't believe he would voluntarily leave his life and his loved ones. He obviously still considered himself bracketed in this group.

The article changed tack and went on to ask rhetorically whether the fact that Matt no longer lived with Kevin just blocks away from the pool in Prahran had any consequences in consideration of his disappearance from the pool? For example, how had Matt got to the pool on that day? Normally he would walk through the park at the rear of the Prahran terrace and then through the backstreets to the pool. His flat in Hawthorn was a good fifteen or twenty minutes drive away (his car, though, was found in the carport out the back) or an indirect trip on public transport incorporating two trams. The question was answered even as it was asked, as it was reported that Matt's friend, Gil, had in fact picked Matt up and driven him to the pool that day.

'Did you pick Matt up that day?' I asked RT. He was sitting across from me reading another section of the paper.

'What?' he asked. He looked at what I was reading, which he had obviously looked at before me. 'Pick him up? Yeah,' he then said and looked back down at his own paper.

Gil, the article went on to say, was 'unavailable for comment', which sounded kind of ominous. Especially as he was sitting next to me.

It was around about that exact moment that I finally twigged why Red Trunks had been getting and studiously ignoring so many calls to his mobile. It must have been the media chasing yet another 'comment'.

I had another jolt of that VIP feeling after this realisation, I admit. It was like RT and me were hiding out from the media at Sharon's Place, and that therefore I was an accessory after the fact or something. For a second it felt all delicious and naughty and made our funked-up little love-nest even more Bonnie and Clyde cosy.

But back to the article. In all, this second interview with Kevin was pretty much the first time since the missing swimmer story broke that there was a definite whiff of suspicion around those involved. We were left with the impression that those most intimate with Matt might actually be a bit dodgy and, in some unspecified and so far not actually understood way, might in fact be responsible for Matt's disappearance.

After that bland line about Gil being 'unavailable for comment' and Kevin having 'lied', Kevin was then asked, surely a little suggestively, where he himself had been on the afternoon Matt had gone missing.

He was, he said blandly in return, 'Working from home' and I could just hear him closing down stonily as he said it.

Home was, the journo reminded us, just a couple of streets away from the pool.

After the 'working from home' article, Kevin did a follow-up interview on the gay radio station Joy FM, and I happened to hear it. Perhaps a little wounded by his treatment at the hands of the mainstream press, a lot more came out in this interview than in his previous one. That is, he was perhaps a little more truthful about the exact nature of the relationship he and Matt shared. You know how conventionally you don't speak ill of the dead? Well, you also don't speak ill of the missing unless it looks like the mainstream press are gunning for you and in that case a little ill- but honest-speaking may be quite appropriate.

In short, the latest revelation was that Kevin and Matt had been in an open relationship for the last year. According to Kevin their relationship went the way of many others—there was nothing, as such, actually wrong with it, they didn't fight, they didn't argue, they hadn't been unfaithful to each other or anything, the relationship had simply degenerated until there didn't seem to be anything left there at all.

'And yet you stayed together. Why?'

'Well because you do. If you've got your lives and your finances all tied up together and there isn't any catastrophe to make you leave, well then you stay. We just stayed.'

As Kevin told it, he was always interested in working through the problems in their relationship, even if these 'problems' seemed only to be boredom and apathy. He suggested one time around the middle of the year that they go to couples counselling and get their partnership back on track, but Matt went once, did not seem interested or hopeful of an outcome, and refused to go again. Matt, Kevin said, had been uninterested either in the relationship or in trying to do anything about it.

'I asked him if he wanted to leave. He said he didn't. I asked him if he wanted to try and work it out, talk to me about it, you know? He said he didn't think there was anything to say. I asked him what he did want, then. And he said he didn't know. He just said he didn't' know. It wasn't particularly helpful.'

In the end Kevin had suggested that in order to force some forward movement, maybe one of them should move out for a while and they should have a proper break. And so the 'open relationship' became a relationship on 'a break', which is where they had got to, with Matt moving out to his flat in Hawthorn, just before the disappearance. It all sounded like the most drawn out way to break up to me, but there you go. Who am I to give relationship advice?

Of course the other revelation in the Joy FM interview was all the sexual stuff. I mean, if you decide to have an 'open relationship'

the implication is that one or both of the partners is seeking sex outside the partnership. Kevin, bless him and his little rimless glasses, hardly seemed the type to dish the dirt on this subject and he didn't. However, he did let a bit slip. As he told it (and you know, I wasn't 100% sure that you could always believe one side of the story without hearing the other, and in this case how could we do that?) there had been no intimacy as such in his relationship with

Matt for pretty much the whole of the year before his disappearance, and that during that time Matt, who had always had quite an appetite in that direction, 'had been visiting sex-on-premises venues regularly.'

The details of the Joy FM interview were picked up by the mainstream press and the big story was that Matt, previously gay poster boy, was actually frequenting sex-on-premises venues engaging in who-knew-what dangerous activities. The underlying message was that this quiet, settled, nice-guy mainstream suburban front had been a sham, and that the seamier life of open relationships and sex-on-premises venues was the truth. It all seemed a bit dark and horrible when really of course it was no such thing.

In any case, this article was pretty much like a starter's pistol for Matt's sexual partners and they tripped over each other coming out of the woodwork. One tabloid headline said it all, I HAD SEX WITH MISSING SWIMMER and underneath it was the story of not one, not two, but three men claiming to have had sex with Matt Gray at a sex-on-premises venue in the city. No one seemed to doubt that these men were telling the truth, and they probably were, although there was no proof to substantiate their stories, but none had anything of interest to tell the police (let alone the reader) about Matt or his disappearance.

And so, just like the previous week, Matt Gray was again all over the place in the media. I saw one lurid letter to the editor that denounced homosexuality entirely and suggested that there was something biblical about Matt's disappearance. Were they allowed to print that sort of shit? There was also a high-handed moralistic opinion piece about sex and its place in society. And there was a sadly thoughtful piece about the degeneration of marriage, which used Matt's relationship as evidence that even gay marriage was susceptible to suburban malaise.

These stories of the missing swimmer's private life and sexual habits seemed to take a long time to go away. Why were we caring so much about this stuff? And why were we being so nasty about it? It seemed very much as if having built Matt up into a whiter-than-white poster boy for Gay Australia we seemed to suddenly have an insatiable appetite for stories that muddied this image. I mean, the fact that Matt was only a poster boy due to the media didn't seem to occur to anyone. Mute and missing, he had been adopted by the public and moulded into something he never was and had no say in. They had created their monster and now they wanted to stone the fucker. The whole thing was just as irrational as the Renaissance chick's dirty ermine.

Ironically, during the days these stories were circulating, RT and I were fucking like rabbits. Sometimes Sharon's Place was absolutely rank with the stink of us, so I'd leave the balcony door open when we went to the pool to air the place out.

*

The eastern edge of the Prahran pool, the edge alongside the aqua painted bleachers, is where all the A-List boys congregate on the hottest days, the boys with the most gym toned tits and arms, a couple with abs so freakishly defined it looks like CGI. They range themselves along the edge of the pool, cooling their heels, sunning their broad chests, looking at each other, and at perfect vantage to be looked at by others. There's usually a lot of big name-brand swimwear worn in this group. Lots of Aussie Bum—do any straight men wear them? Or maybe Versace briefs with a camp little white belt at the top through tiny belt loops. With the swimwear and the abs there is usually a fair amount of baseball caps and sunglasses—aviators are popular, but the big plastic bug-eyes still get a work-out. There might be a bit of cheek-kissing as newcomers come down to the water's edge and join those already there, and there'll be more cheek-kissing as someone gets up, rearranges his dick in his togs and returns to wherever he was sunning himself. There's lots of coming and going at the water's edge, preening and splashing, and all the while the boys cackle and chatter and laugh together like gym-built hyenas. It's like a scene from some nature show. You know, the one right before the lions attack.

One day, a few days into the backlash, it was hot, above 40 degrees, so I sat amongst the A-list boys, which I normally didn't do, and I heard some of the things they were chattering about. Mostly it was about plans for the weekend. Or what they'd done on NYE. Where they went, how much they got their ticket for and what they spent on drugs. There were conversations about boyfriends, about friends and friends of friends and friends of friend's new boyfriends. About hook-ups from the previous weekend and possibilities for this weekend. About where they'd been for their holidays and how much it had cost and what the hotel was like. About property that had just been bought or just been sold. About gym. About running. About swimming. About triathlons. But mostly about gym. Occasionally there was someone talking about something, well something not gay, but they were in the minority of a minority. Then again, you don't go and sit in the gayest spot of the gayest pool in Melbourne with a whole lot of other gay men and not talk about gay things.

The guy sitting right next to me was saying something that I guessed was about the missing swimmer.

'Oh they'll find him soon enough,' he said. He was talking to two companions who stood in the water in front of him. 'In someone's backyard, or out in the bush somewhere in a shallow grave,' he finished.

One companion said, 'Eeuw.' The other said, 'You really think so?'

'They always turn up dead sooner or later,' the first guy said.

This comment floored them for a while and they were silent, heads back, chins up, turning blank sunglasses from left to right. After a moment or two of this though, the 'eeuw' boy, who seemed kind of ditzy but sweet, started up again.

'You know Jeremy? Well he goes to that sex-on-premises place in the city. What's it called? On Lonsdale?'

'Oh, like you don't know,' his friend in the pool next to him said lazily.

'And he said he saw this guy, this Matt guy there. A couple of times he said he saw him.'

'Did he do him?' the first guy asked. I didn't like this first guy much. He was an asshole.

'I don't know. I didn't ask.'

'With Jeremy you wouldn't have to ask,' said his mate in the pool.

'I s'pose a lot of people had sex with him there. Jeremy wouldn't be the only one. I mean, I heard he's been doing the saunas for months.'

'Oh well, you know, people do it.'

'Of course,' the 'euuw' boy said. 'It's just that, I suppose it's funny to see it in the paper. You know?'

'The papers are loving it,' the first guy said, in a shitty, knowing kind of way, like he was personally dirty on the newspapers. The others agreed and both went 'yeah' in a similar kind of way. They seemed suddenly like school boys in a footy team talking about an umpiring decision they thought was unfair. It was a team-gay kind of comment, as if the fact the papers were reporting that Matt visited sex-on-premises venues was like a crap umpiring decision. Perhaps in a way they were right.

I had a conversation (well, a kind of conversation) about this issue with RT earlier in the week, when the stories about Matt and his sex-capades outside his relationship with Kevin first came out.

We were having brekky, reading the papers, when RT said he took issue with the way Matt was being represented in the press. What he actually said was, 'You know I hate this fucking paper.'

He was looking at the letters to the editor page where they also showed the results of a questionnaire from the previous day. They run these stupid poll things on these dumb questions that it's obvious what the answer's gunna be. Things like, Do you think paedophiles should have their dicks chopped off? Or do you think petrol should be cheaper? Or something lame like that. And then surprise surprise, the next day there's this big red graph line, or blue or whatever, and everyone's answered exactly as you would have expected. I mean, couldn't they choose a question on an issue that's actually divisive, or a little subtle? Apparently not. Instead they blatantly appeal to this lowest common denominator of dumb conventional people and stir up their dumb conventional attitudes and regurgitate it all back to them. It's kind of depressing to think there's this big, fat soup of dumb people out there who'll SMS in to answer that dumb fucking question.

'You mean all the letters about Matt?' I asked.

He just grunted, neither yes or no precisely, but of course that's exactly what it was about. The turn-around. Last week Matt was poster boy for gay marriage and the soup loved him. But this week, they find out he regularly had sex outside his partnership with Kevin at saunas and he's now this sex-crazed AIDS fucker whose lifestyle obviously had something to do with him going missing, and bang, everyone's nodding smarmily to themselves and thinking what they're supposed to think and the graph's gone totally the other way and people are judging him without knowing him properly, or what he was like or anything. I guess it's the crowd mentality, like birds swooping together in the sky or dozens of mopeds rounding a corner into a square in Barcelona.

I looked at RT for a bit. He sat there frowning in concentration like he was practicing some mesmerist-type trick and the newspaper would any second spontaneously combust.

'It's like having a sexual appetite is wrong,' he said after a moment of two. 'I mean, we all fuck, don't we?'

I said that he and I had definitely been doing our own fair share of it recently.

He said it was just a pity it all sounded so filthy. And he's got a point. Bring all the sex-on-premises stuff out into the light of day and it does kind of seem a bit sex-piggy and filthy to Mr and Mrs Average don't you think? Even I can see that. Don't get me wrong, I don't mind a bit of filthy sex-piggery occasionally myself but I can see how it looks when it's dragged out into the harsh light of day and served up cold to us with our OJ. But wouldn't all sorts of sexual behaviour seem the same? Don't we all have a sexual side of us which isn't meant for public consumption? I mean, just because you and your girlfriend are on best behaviour on a visit to grandma doesn't mean she's not going to give you a head-job in the car on the way home. (Your girlfriend, not grandma.) Just because they're your parents, doesn't mean they don't fuck like rabbits whenever they get the chance. And gay men, they fuck each other up the ass, you know, and have anonymous sex in saunas, I've heard. Sex happens everywhere, but behind closed doors, in bedrooms, down little side-streets, and in dark cubicles up anonymous stairways. How many people would be comfortable with their sexual history being reported in the press? Maybe some CCTV footage? Not many. Not in Australia anyhow. I think about Big Brother in Brazil and some of the Scandinavian countries, and the contestants in those countries seem much more comfortable with sex, masturbating and even fucking in front of the cameras, apparently happy for it to be broadcast to a large audience. But Australia isn't like that. Australia is, by and large, a conservative country, where Big Brother contestants masturbate and copulate, if at all, secretly, under the doona.

The truth to me seemed to be that Matt was just a normal guy with a normal sexual appetite. That is he wanted sex. Not heaps of sex, but some, regularly, and when his relationship with Kevin stopped being sexual, he went elsewhere for it. It was actually quite simple. Natural. Normal. Those sorts of words.

Perhaps at first Matt hadn't been totally honest with Kevin about playing away, but maybe he was safe and discreet which is at least the next best thing. Their partnership must have seemed more like an arrangement than a relationship for a couple of years by that stage, as if they shared their lives, but didn't share themselves. Shared property. Shared time. Shared bed. Shared tasks. Shared stuff. But nothing more than that any longer. Matt was all for ending the relationship. He wanted a clean break, both emotionally and financially. But Kevin wanted to hold on. It was Kevin who suggested the open relationship and Matt seeking sex outside their partnership, Kevin who suggested they get couples counselling, talk over the issues in their relationship and try to 'work things out'. Of all the doom-laden writing-on-the-wall phrases.

'Did Matt tell you he was moving out?' I asked RT.

'Yeah. He told me.'

'And what did you say?'

He put his paper down and looked at me.

'I congratulated him.'

'Really?'

'Yeah. He'd been to-ing and fro-ing about it for months. I was getting sick of hearing about it to tell you the truth. So I congratulated him on finally making up his mind. But he wasn't sure at all. He said he had no idea what he was doing.'

'I see,' I said carefully. I felt the plot thickening ever so slightly.

'Are we going to the pool or what?' RT then asked in a subject-closed kind of way.

*

Oh, one other thing. Before we left for the pool that day, I accidentally found Mr T's hidey-hole of smut. It was in the bedroom cupboard underneath the bottom drawer. You had to pull it out completely, as I accidentally did one day, obviously not knowing my own strength, to find the space. And just as I had suspected, it was gay porn. The dirty bugger had been gay all along. All this denying it and dates with women and saying things like 'I really appreciate my gay fans, but I'm not gay', and I find Bel Ami DVDs in his porn stash. Well well well.

I called my sister and told her that 1) I was OK and 2) Mr T was gay.

5

As far as headlines go it had all the verve of a limp dick. MISSING SWIMMER: LOVER COMES FORWARD. I mean, it wasn't exactly breaking news considering that over the last week or so men who'd had sex with Matt had joined arms and high-kicked in formation for the media, like a chorus line of slutty Vegas Showgirls, dishing the details and elbowing each other aside for their own fifteen seconds of media notoriety. Whatever interest there had been had well and truly and very quickly dried up. We got the idea, you know, that Matt was fucking around.

So why that headline? After a quick glance at the article it appeared that Matt had found himself a new partner. There was a picture of this new partner accompanying the article and the first thing I thought when I saw it was, No way. His name was Noah and he looked like a complete nerd. He had a pasty, uncooked-hamburger kind of face, not much of a chin, a snaggle-toothed mouth and floppy dark hair. Just looking at him (and I know this is totally superficial but we all do it) I just couldn't believe that Matt would be interested in him. Matt was all clean-cut and popular and outdoorsy, and this other guy looked like he was into *Star Trek* and spent hours wanking around online. But then, and simply because he was everything the smart and handsome Kevin wasn't, just like RT was the exact opposite of Leo, I suddenly knew it could be true and believed in it absolutely, because of rather than in spite of this Noah guy's plug-ugly mug.

The Noah guy told us first a bit about how he and Matt met and how long they'd been together. It seemed they met at the sex-on-premises venue, which was not such a surprise, as we'd seen from the conga-line, but it was in the sense that these venues don't usually lead to a life-long love match. However they met there a few times for sex, then eventually got talking and decided to take it outside.

Matt apparently talked with this Noah guy a lot about his life. About how hollow everything felt, how he'd had enough of a life of consuming, just working to earn money to buy more things he didn't really want and didn't get any pleasure out of, feeding more and more money into a suburban life that he didn't feel was him. He was a sad man, Noah thought, or at least a man who had come to a sad place.

'But he was positive about the future,' he was quoted as saying. 'Hopeful, I think. Especially after we got together.'

I rolled my eyes. What a simper that line was.

The article went on to say ominously that Noah was 'helping the police with their enquires'. The journalist asked Noah exactly what that meant.

Noah said that they had taken him to Matt's new flat in Hawthorn to see if he had any comments that might help.

'I wasn't able to help them though. I mean, there was nothing much to see. He'd only just moved in so there was hardly anything there. In the lounge room there was just a huge wide screen TV. Nothing else. It wasn't even plugged in. And he was still living out of a suitcase.'

He also took them to his own place. Matt had stayed there a few times and he'd given them some things he'd left there. Nothing much, just some clothes.

The journalist then asked about the mystery blond man Matt was seen speaking to at the Prahran pool on the day of his disappearance.

But Noah didn't have any idea about that. He said that Matt had kept him from any friends of his, completely separate from his old life. He wanted a fresh start, he said, just the two of them.

'And on the day that Matt disappeared, where were you?'

'At work.'

He worked for a local council in some archiving capacity, which seemed, looking at him, entirely believable. He wouldn't, generally speaking, be the sort of person you'd put front-of-house.

On the question of what he thought happened to Matt he said he didn't know.

'It saddens me, but I just don't know. I know he wanted out of his life as it was, he wanted change, but I just can't believe he'd disappear of his own free will and not contact me if he was able to. If he could get to a phone, or even to a computer, he would call me or email me or even send me a letter or a postcard or something. I know he would. We had become very close over the last few months. We would talk about all the things he wanted to do, and that we could do in the future. I can't help but feel that, well that this isn't a voluntary disappearance, as people are starting to say in the papers. No, I think that there are others involved and that he's been taken.'

The journalist asked him what exactly he meant by 'taken'. I think I knew what was in the journo's mind. Was he talking about alien abduction or what? But apparently Noah had become too distressed to answer the question and say exactly what he had meant. When he calmed down he was quoted as saying something quite cryptic, which kind of closed the subject for now. He said that all he knew was that Matt wasn't dead. He knew it in his heart. 'Matt is out there somewhere.'

Yeah, I thought, just like the truth is out there. Who was this freak? Although I suppose it isn't necessarily so freaky for the family and friends of missing people to believe blindly, no matter what the evidence points to, that their loved one is still out there somewhere. Again and again you read about it or saw it on the news with tearful family members making pleas, and somehow, you knew, deep down, that whoever it was who was gone was dead and that they'd never come back. And yet you knew also that if it was you in their place you would believe just as fiercely as them. Nothing short of a body and a burial would make you stop believing.

Matt Gray wasn't dead yet.

When I showed RT the article, he read it, raised his eyebrows in a disbelieving kind of way and said, 'I wouldn't have thought he was Matt's type.'

'What was Matt's type?' I asked.

RT shrugged.

I wondered suddenly just how much RT cared for Matt. I wondered, too, just then, right at that moment, whether or not he'd ever slept with Matt. Look, it's the sort of thing that would slip into your mind too, I bet, so I'm not apologising for it. Even so, there was no way I was actually going to ask him. Certainly not right then. RT finally got around to asking me about Sharon's Place. For a week or so it didn't seem to occur to him to wonder how I, with no job and no income and from everything I'd said about my past, having never had a great income, could be living in a three-bedroom apartment on the Docklands, full of beige furnishings and yucca plants.

So yeah, I told him the story about my sister being in real estate in Sydney and how she came to the rescue when I got back from Spain and got me this apartment-sitting thing. I also told him that it actually belonged to a man who was famous and also, I had discovered due to my incredible stealth and subterfuge, secretly gay, or at least that he had a secret stash of Bel Ami DVDs which was kind of the same thing.

RT then played totally into my hands by demanding to be told who owned the flat, but of course I told him I was sworn to secrecy and would never tell him. Then he guessed a few stupid guesses, but when guessing randomly didn't work he started in with the twenty questions.

'Is he a soap star?'

'No.'

'Was he on *Australian Idol?*'

'No.'

'Is he on the tele?'

'Yes, but he's not an actor.'

'Is he a sportsman?'

'Yes.'

'A-ha!'

After a few more wrong guesses, RT grew bored of the game and just wanted me to tell him who it was. He tried pleading, then used an honest-to-God just tell me kind of tack, then got school-masterly and stern. Finally he tried tickling, but that turned into wrestling and that turned into kissing and that turned into sex and by then the subject was closed.

Or I thought it was. A little later, when we were snuggling up together on the couch he asked in a small voice half muffled by my shoulder.

'What DVDs were they?'

So of course I got them out and we made a night of it.

×

The next day we were back at the pool. While RT was off doing his laps, I moved our gear a step up, chasing the retreating shade, so that when he came back from his laps he could still be out of the sun. I made a rueful face at myself for being such a little surfie chick, minding his towel and all.

When RT did come back he'd obviously done more than his usual number of laps because apart from looking pleased with himself he looked more exhausted. His cheeks were flushed and his breath came a bit quicker. His eyes had goggle-marks around them and his hair was wet. He was all loose-limbed and pumped up.

He wiped himself down a bit and sat on his towel on the step above me, as carefully out of the sun as I was in it. I smiled and lay down on my back, putting my teeshirt over my face.

'How many?' I asked.

'Forty freestyle. Ten kickboard.'

'More than usual.'

'U-huh,' he said.

I thought, like you do with RT, that it was all over. I mean, that's what conversations, if that's not too fine a word, are like with him. But after a bit, and I mean about ten minutes, he went on.

'You know Matt said to me once, he said he wondered how far he'd swum.'

His voice came from above me, somewhere on the other side of the teeshirt-darkness. It was disembodied and sounded a bit different. I don't know how. Pensive? Reminiscent? I don't know the word.

'All together,' he clarified. 'He said, If all the laps I'd ever done were in a straight line, how far would I have swum?'

Another pause. Silence. Yes? Was he going to go on?

'How did he mean?' I asked. My voice sounded in my ears like an earache.

'Well,' RT went on after a moment. 'He did, say, 30 laps a day of the 50 metre pool. So 1.5k a day around 5 days a week. Which adds up to ... whatever it adds up to.'

'7.5k,' I said.

'Right. Yeah. So he swims 7.5k a week, and he's been swimming that regularly for the last year, say. That's 56 weeks. Some more, some less, maybe, but he said it'd all even out. So that's ... what is that a year?'

I sat up on my elbows and took the teeshirt off my face. The sun was blinding after so long, and I squinted up at RT who sat above me in the shade.

'About 400k,' I said after a few tick-tocks of thinking time. 'A bit more. 420k.'

'So he worked out that he'd swum 420k in the last year,' RT

said. He was gazing vaguely out over the pool. 'I mean, he worked it out exactly. Whatever it was. And then next time we met, he'd been into a road directory and, you know, worked out exactly where he could have swum to if all his laps were in a straight line. He worked out that he could have got to some place called … I can't remember. It started with A. Apsley, I think.'

I turned away from RT and looked out over the pool as he did. I could see him. Matt I mean. I could see him all dreamy about the idea, and really into it, just like RT had described. Adding up his laps, maybe writing down figures with a pencil on a little jotter or pad or something. Then opening up a map of Victoria and working it out. Maybe with a ruler or a piece of string, working out distances, perhaps as the crow flies, or between towns via the highways. And finding himself at Apsley. Wherever that was.

'Never heard of it,' I said.

'Me neither,' RT said, reverting to his usual disinterested tone. 'Do you want a Coke?'

We stayed at the pool a long time that afternoon, made a real good session of it, and left just before closing time at 7.30. Afterwards we went for a steak and a few beers at a pub close by. It was early in the week and it was pretty dead, but kind of nice. We were all hot and lazy, and a bit fucked to tell the truth after last night and Mr T's porn. At one point, feeling like this, all lazy, and after a few beers, RT started talking about Matt again. He wasn't exactly slurring his words, but he wasn't really making proper sentences either. He was just talking. Staring at the open fire, which of course wasn't lit, talking to it, or to me, or to Matt or whatever. I can't quite remember exactly the words he used, but he started by saying how much Matt loved his laps. How he loved getting in and just going for it. He could spend forever just doing laps. RT said that one time he'd asked Matt what he thought about when he swum his laps and Matt had said, Nothing. He'd said that was the point. That was why it was so good. It made him feel centred, he said. And calm.

'Somehow he loved the idea that laps were forever,' RT said. 'Just a tumble turn and another lap. Keep going.'

We both stared into the unlit fireplace for a bit then. I was thinking about that little A-town that Matt had said he'd swum to. Apsley. I'd never heard of it, but 420 kilometres would take you from Melbourne to the borders of Victoria or into New South Wales somewhere. I don't think you'd get across the border into South Australia but maybe if you went directly across you would. Of course, if you were swimming it you could also get across to Tassie. Apsley could be anywhere. I'm not sure why, but in the back of my head I felt maybe that this had implications of some kind for Matt's disappearance. But what? How? Where was this Apsley? How big was it? Were there motels there where a stranger could come and hide out? But then I clicked it was an entirely stupid idea. If Matt was of a mind to voluntarily disappear, why on earth would he go to some little place based on how many kilometres he'd swum that year. It was a dumb idea.

I nudged RT. We needed to get moving, so we wandered back through the streets, past one of those big hi-rise commission flats, through a dusty little abandoned park, towards Malvern Road and the tram home. This brought us close by the pool and we stopped there for a moment, hanging on with our fingers through the wire of the fence. It was dark and the pool was of course closed and empty of people, but it wasn't covered or lit. It was just sitting there in the dark waiting for the next day. The surface was perfectly still and reflected the black of the sky and one or two of the lamps in the park behind us.

'Listen,' RT said in a whisper. 'Can you hear that?'

I listened but couldn't hear anything.

Then, after a while, bit by bit I heard it. Splashing. Not big splashing, like someone doing a bomb or something, but gentle rhythmic splashing, like someone doing laps.

I shook my head at him and let go of the wire fence.

'It's just the filtration system,' I said.

*

Back at Sharon's Place RT started in on me about Mr T again.

'So he's a sportsman?'

'Well, he *was*.'

'And he's on the tele.'

'Well, he was when he was a sportsman and being interviewed and stuff. Not so much now.'

'What's he doing now?'

'I don't know actually. I guess he's retired.'

'And how old is he?'

'I think still in his 20s. Maybe 30s by now.'

'And he's hot?'

'Shit hot.'

'He was in the Sydney Olympics wasn't he?'

'Mmm, might have been.'

'I know who it is.'

'Yeah, who.'

'I know exactly who it is.'

'You do not.'

'I do.'

'You're just saying that. You've got no idea.'

Pause.

'What's your sister's phone number?' RT asked.

'I'm not giving that to you.'

His eyes flickered down to the coffee table. He was looking for something. My phone! I launched myself off the couch and ran through Sharon's Place, scrambling on the rugs and grabbing the door frames, rounding corners on two wheels, until finally I launched onto my phone which was on the floor beside the bed and hoed it into the ground like a rugby tackle. Only seconds behind me, RT launched himself too, except he was a whole lot heavier than me and the big fucker knocked the wind out of me and jammed my head into the floor so that it felt like it went a whole other shape, like a balloon. After his jump tackle I felt woozy, but knew I'd be fine, however RT was sorry and got off me and asked if I was OK and examined my head and was solicitous. Anyhow, to cut to the chase, we had sex again.

*

Our little friend Noah was in the papers again the next day. I didn't know whether to be disgusted with his media-slut ways, or grudgingly impressed with him for making it

80

last, you know? I mean, he seemed earnest and heartfelt, but he was also milking his connection to Matt like crazy.

I think the funniest thing about the rise and rise (to that point) of Noah, was the way the whole UFO thing dogged him. I mean to be fair he never once said anything about literally believing Matt was abducted by aliens, and yet the majority of the public I'm sure will remember him as the freak who believed a UFO took the missing swimmer.

It all started, of course, with that unfortunate comment in his first interview that he believed Matt 'was taken'. Innocent enough. But then there was a follow-up article in the gay press a day or two later, which was illustrated with a picture of Noah taken in front of the Prahran pool. The photographer, who was either perfectly innocent or a sneaky little shit with a sense of humour, made sure to be slightly below Noah and took a photo of him looking pensively off to the side and up into the sky. Sure enough, when the picture appeared, Noah's comment that Matt had been 'taken' was printed underneath it. In the article itself he said pretty much more of what he'd already said in his other interview, however it was that pensive look up into the blank skies with 'He was taken' underneath it that people remembered and commented on.

The first actual mention of alien abduction in connection with Matt Gray I personally saw in the media was in a review of *Coneheads* which was showing at the Rooftop Cinema. Their online review said something along the lines of, 'Fresh from their recent appearance at the Prahran swimming pool ...'

After this I think there was next an editorial that used Noah's (supposed) belief that Matt was abducted by aliens as a jumping off point for a discussion of the many bizarre urban legends that surround mysterious happenings in Australia's history. The journo believed that the very fact something was considered 'unsolved' created an instant void which resulted in the human mind rushing to create an answer, as there was something in our nature that needed answers and routines and known quantities. And because there was infinite variety in the human mind, there were as many bizarre explanations for unsolved happenings as there were people who believed completely and devotedly in them. It was actually quite an interesting idea and a well-written editorial, but it in turn led to a flurry of communication in the Letters to the Editor page, all just that little bit further off the point and now squarely on the subject of UFOs. Most letters ridiculed the whole idea, but amazingly some people also wrote in to say they 'supported Noah'.

It was after a day or two of this that there was another interview with Noah in which he took the time to make the point he'd never actually said anything about believing Matt's disappearance was an alien abduction and that people 'should not take my ideas and beliefs out of context.'

Now, this struck me at the time as somewhat, well, ambiguous? But as the days wore on I realised that it was a very careful manoeuvre. At one point, and I can't remember now where I heard this, maybe on morning radio, Noah walked a wonderful tightrope something like, 'I can't believe so much is being said about me believing Matt has been abducted by a UFO.'

'So, can I ask if you do believe in UFOs?'

'Look I just refuse to comment on that when there are so many more serious things to discuss about Matt's disappearance.' It was brilliant really, and given the newsworthiness of what Noah actually had to say about Matt and the circumstances of his disappearance, which was in effect nothing, the constantly bubbling UFO angle ensured things stayed in the news just that extra few days, enough to make it a proper nine-day wonder.

Of course RT took the view that this Noah joker was just making a mockery of Matt's disappearance and that it was wasting valuable time and attention. When RT expressed this opinion I listened with a very serious face, then nodded and said contritely that he was, of course, right, but I swear at that moment I could have thrown my Fruit Loops right at his head. I mean, I was just enjoying a bit of abstract thinking about the nature of nine-day wonders and he had to go and make it all personal on me.

6

Being a man of little imagination and a lover of routine, every morning RT would get up late morning, shuffle out to the little supermarket downstairs to get the papers, then return to bed where he would stay for an hour or two reading them. One day I had the brilliant idea that I would go to the shop and get the papers for him while he was asleep. I did this and he promptly asked if I could please not because he enjoyed the walk after waking up and missed having a chat with the Supermarket girl. This being the skank, by the way, who hated my guts after the Skittles thing. And also, a chat? RT? I'd never known anyone less chatty. He barely spoke to me. He barely spoke to anyone. What could he talk to this woman about? Anyhow, I was daily reminded of our incompatibility so this latest example was not exactly a newsflash. Although perhaps I don't mean incompatibility as such, just that we had very little in common. Or is that exactly the same thing?

In fact, if I think about it there were only ever two things we had in common; we enjoyed an incredible sexual compatibility and we both thought Nicole Kidman was going to someday go completely off the planet. We discussed this on the tram one day and it's a theory I must admit I'm still particularly keen on. I can just see it, can't you? After one too many botox injections Our Nic gets an eye twitch and goes into hiding in a fabulous mansion on some Greek Island or something, stalking around with a big sunhat and black glasses, perhaps with a little bandaid across her nose or something, and always wearing white gloves, snipping off the heads of flowers, listening to something no one else can hear, and refusing to allow the gardener have his children play on the grass for some unspecified reason. I could go on, but I think you get the picture.

Come to think of it Red Trunks did nothing more than agree with me absent-mindedly after I outlined my Nic scenario. I'm beginning to suspect he wasn't even listening, in which case we only really had one thing in common.

But yeah, the point is I let him buy the papers. I also took to going back to bed with him while he read them, and so it was that at 2 pm one afternoon we were in bed together, eating sticky Danishes and reading the papers. It sounds hedonistic, but in reality I felt vaguely lazy and guilty, like a dole-bludger.

There hadn't been anything much about the missing swimmer in the papers for a few days, maybe even a full week, since all the Noah shit. But out of the blue one day there was an article entitled POOL MYSTERY DEEPENS. Not a bad pun for News Limited. However, the link to Matt this time was a tenuous one at best. Basically there was a charred corpse found in a factory fire in Kensington and the question was asked, Had the missing swimmer been found?

Kensington is an inner city suburb in the inner North West. It's on the opposite side of Melbourne city to the suburb of Prahran and is only a suburb or two away from Sharon's Place. It's an interesting little suburb, half low-key industrial, half residential, but gentrifying day by day. The Melbourne stockyards used to be there, but now the stockyards are gone and there are huge amounts of new townhouses where once cows got the chop.

Anyhow, a warehouse in a back street in Kensington burnt to the ground in the middle of the night. The blaze was not considered to be deliberately lit or suspicious as such. The warehouse was unused and dilapidated, and at the back, via one of those skinny old bluestone alleyways you find around the inner suburbs, some of the cladding was broken off, providing access to the warehouse. A number of homeless people used it as a place to doss down.

After firemen had been and extinguished the blaze, which burnt intensely due to the old fashioned building materials and bolts of material which were stored in one area, they revealed that they had discovered a body, a very badly charred corpse. It did not look like the man (for it seemed to be the body of a man) had been conscious at the time of the blaze as there was no indication he had tried to escape. The most obvious presumption, of course, was that the victim was one of the homeless people who were sleeping there and that either he was asleep or drunk or doped up or something and just died without trying to save himself. However given they'd had no time to properly investigate, the police were unable to confirm either the identity or the actual cause of death.

So where does the connection to the missing swimmer come in? Basically because the body was three things; male, around the right age, and unidentified. Oh, and then there was the fact that the corpse was, apparently, wearing plastic thongs. They were melted but still identifiable as plastic thongs. White plastic thongs.

Was Matt wearing thongs the day he disappeared? If so, were they white thongs? If so, could this body could be his? That seemed to be the gist of the story. As tenuous as this link seemed, apparently the police were seeking more information about what footwear Matt Gray was wearing on the day of his disappearance.

To begin with, the article revisited witness accounts from the day. But either people hadn't really noticed what Matt was wearing on his feet, or they just presumed he was wearing thongs. As for the colour of these thongs, if his mates didn't particularly notice that he was wearing them, they wouldn't be likely to notice the colour, and unsurprisingly none of the witnesses had mentioned at the time, nor could confirm now, the colour of Matt's thongs. In which case he could have been wearing a white pair, couldn't he? Well, yes. Did he, in fact, have a white pair? Kevin when asked said that Matt had owned a number of pairs of thongs, about three perhaps, of different colours, one of which he was sure was white. Paul agreed that Matt had a couple of pairs of thongs and that one was white. (I presumed that Gil had been 'unavailable for comment' again, bless him.) The police had then apparently searched Matt's Hawthorn flat and found a brown pair and a red pair of thongs, but no white pair. So the conclusion was that like the majority of Australian men on a nearly 40 degree day Matt was wearing thongs. And yeah, they were probably white. But so what? It didn't mean he was the white-thong-wearing corpse in the Kensington warehouse.

Even at the time I never much believed in the missing-swimmer-as-charred-corpse story. No, to me the freakier aspect to the whole white-thong angle on the missing swimmer story was the fact they were missing in the first place. There was something in that, I was sure.

After the disappearance, Matt's bag and towel were found right where he had left them on the aqua steps, but no thongs were found with his belongings, nor were any discovered anywhere around the pool or in the changerooms that day. The implication seems obvious. Wherever Matt disappeared to that day he was wearing his green and white striped togs, carrying his goggles and wearing his white thongs. But if you think about it, there's a bit missing in there. The last time Matt was seen was around 2.20 pm diving into the pool, or if you believe RT's sighting at 3.22 pm precisely, doing a tumble turn in the fast lane. In either case, patently not in a position to be wearing white plastic thongs. So he can't have been wearing them. And yet they were missing from the Prahran pool just as much as Matt was, which means there's a bit in there we knew nothing about.

It was precisely the time-slip, wormhole, rip-in-time moment I was looking for and I felt suddenly like I'd seen the whole thing from a perspective that somehow would make everything clear if I just thought about it harder. The rest of them, ha, they were way off track with this charred corpse in thongs bullshit, but I had come up with something really important.

However, the more I tried to clarify in my own head what this discovery meant, the more it was like waking up from a dream— abstractly it felt like the mystery of the universe had been unlocked, and yet all I could actually really remember was running down a street in my pyjamas which didn't seem all that profound

*

I couldn't stop thinking about Matt's flat in Hawthorn. That article, that white-thong article said that the police had searched Matt's flat, and that got me thinking, because by that time we were about a month down the track from the disappearance, which meant that all his stuff had been locked up in there all that time. I mean, I guess that's normal. I suppose the landlord was hardly going to take all the stuff and leave it on the nature strip. It wasn't like he was dead. Well, not definitely. But I wondered, I just wondered about the rent and how long he was paid up for and what would happen when the rent ran out. I supposed Kevin, or more probably Matt's parents, who I'd only seen once on that tearful press conference, would keep paying the rent month after month. They'd leave all Matt's stuff in there and the air would get really still and begin to smell strongly of the carpet and the furnishing, not of human habitation, and they'd keep paying the rent and waiting for Matt to come back. I couldn't stop thinking about that flat.

*

Of course all this media activity with the charred corpse and everything provided a perfect opportunity for our little friend Noah to poke his pancake head up again. Not qualifying for the big players any longer, he appeared in the gay press under a headline that read, I KNOW MATT IS ALIVE, photographed looking earnest and clutching to his chest a pair of white thongs which were so suspiciously whiter-than-white they'd obviously been purchased new for the photo-op.

Fuck, he made me laugh. Surely he had to be doing all this shit with his tongue in his cheek. He must be taking the piss. Funny, I could in a strange way understand the attraction Matt must have felt for him.

*

Poor Kevin. He got a real hammering the days after the Kensington fire. The charred corpse remained officially unidentified so of course everyone thought it was Matt and that Kevin killed him, dumped his body in the Kensington warehouse and torched it. There were two things that lead to public opinion going so firmly in this direction and casting Kevin in the role of murderer and arsonist. Firstly, a nice classic Agatha Christie style motive came out, then there was that anonymous call to the police.

The motivation? Money of course. Not, it turns out, millions, but does it have to be? Basically, it turned out Matt and Kevin's only joint investment was in the house in Prahran. Outside that, Kevin had ploughed all of his own money into his business, which had, it turned out, hardly been a financial success. Kevin kept pouring what little profit there was back into the business, but it still went nowhere and in fact had gone downhill considerably so that the business was due to fold. Matt, on the other hand, plugged away in his boring old job working for the man, used his income to pay extra off his half of the mortgage, made a few canny investments that had paid well and even more recently purchased an investment rental property.

The upshot was that if Matt and Kevin separated, which of course they were in the early stages of doing, or had already done depending on your definition of the word, and were forced to sell the house in Prahran and pay out the mortgage, Matt would be left quite comfortably off and Kevin, to put it succinctly, would be in deep financial shit.

Adding spice to Kevin's financial motive, and recapped by the helpful media, was Matt's infidelity and sexual activity outside the partnership over the last year prior to his disappearance, the humiliation of the 'open relationship' and the ultimate 'break' they had been on. In short, details of Matt and Kevin's emotional and financial lives were being aired in public like so many cum-stained sheets, and it suddenly didn't seem beyond imagining that Kevin had sufficient motivation to do something brutal.

During all this, Kevin adopted a cold poise and a 'no comment' stance. He'd spoken to the press quite enough thank you and a fat lot of good it had done him. This didn't help and he became in our eyes definitely a suspicious character. There were a number of sightings of him reported or rumoured; he was seen in Kensington in the general vicinity of the warehouse fire, but on the day following (returning to the scene of the crime perhaps?), lurking around a 7-11 in St Kilda (which, correct me if I'm wrong, is actually a totally innocent if not very interesting thing to be doing), and at the Harold Holt public swimming pool (which, other than being 'on theme', actually makes no sense at all if you think about it). He was also seen purchasing petrol in a jerry-can the weekend before the fire, which he actually did do, apparently, but I'd say the 2-stroke was for his lawn mower rather than to use as an accelerant, wouldn't you?

In the end it was reported in a cool-as-ice headline, SWIMMER'S PARTNER FLEES MELBOURNE. He didn't just leave Melbourne, he fled apparently, driven back into the bosom of his retired parents on Queensland's Gold Coast. I felt personally vaguely guilty about it, like I'd gone out to get a DVD from Blockbuster and had somehow unwittingly got caught up in an angry mob carrying torches.

Then there was the anonymous phone call. Almost immediately after Kevin left Melbourne for the Gold Coast a leaked transcript of an anonymous phone call received by the police found its way into the papers. The transcript was short and sweet, but the caller said that he (it was a male voice, slightly disguised) knew for certain that the missing swimmer was 'buried in a backyard in Prahran'.

There were two people connected with the case, the article went on to report, who lived in the suburb of Prahran and while Noah lived in a block of flats without a garden of any type let alone a backyard, Kevin, of course, lived in a terrace with a backyard (not to mention, I thought to myself, a tool shed with lots of garden implements appropriate for grave digging). Although there are presumably millions of other backyards in Prahran, the implication was clear, and suddenly Kevin's trip to the Gold Coast did indeed look like he'd shot through.

The police response to this leak was soggy to say the least. They refused to comment on the anonymous phone call, but did say that since the start of the Matt Gray case they had received an incredible amount of anonymous calls, as they invariably did in this type of high-profile disappearance, and that all information received was logged and would be dealt with in a timely and appropriate manner. This wet blanket statement turned out to be a bit disingenuous though, as only the next day they appeared to be following up on the 'Prahran backyard' lead, and within 24 hours it was reported that they had asked poor Kevin to return to Melbourne to 'assist them with their enquiries', which presumably would include digging up his backyard.

I must admit that as soon as I read about the anonymous call I jumped to the conclusion that Noah had made it. Somehow, I could just imagine him making an anonymous call. He seemed the type, the controversy-courting type who might do something weird like that to stir up trouble or to keep his photo in the paper. Or maybe it was simpler than that. In a way, mention of a backyard turned suspicion off him, as he didn't have a backyard, and onto Kevin who definitely did.

Kevin. Could he have made the call? But why would he? The call implicated him more than anybody. Admittedly, it also seemed to distract attention from the charred corpse. There was another possibility of course. Perhaps the anonymous caller was none other than Matt Gray himself. I mean, there was no evidence he was dead, either charred in a warehouse fire in Kensington or buried in a backyard in Prahran. He could have been alive and well and making calls to the police.

*

I discovered a website where you could vote for what you thought happened to the missing swimmer. The options were: amnesia, voluntary disappearance, suicide, abduction (murder), or abduction (alien). The results of the votes were displayed on a bar graph. The highest number of votes at the time I visited the site was for alien abduction which didn't surprise me in the least. Noah, it seems, was becoming a bit of a star with the online social networking crowd. Figures.

7

Totally unexpectedly, I met the missing swimmer's family. His Mum and Dad and his sister.

RT asked me if I would come with him to a party. I was a bit surprised, I suppose, because our days together up until then had been anything but social, but I said yeah, of course I would.

We were getting ready to go and he was looking all stern and constipated. I waited (drumming my fingers in my head) and soon enough he came clean and told me that the party was kind of weird in that it was for Matt.

'Matt who?' I asked. Not my finest moment we will agree.

Matt the missing swimmer, he told me. It was his birthday and his family wanted to celebrate even though he wasn't there. RT looked embarrassed, then said that he had to go even though it made him uncomfortable, because he'd known Matt since high school and the Grays, he said, had always been very good to him.

Matt Gray's parents lived out in an eastern suburb, further out than the 'leafy' eastern suburbs but not so far as the Dandenong Ranges. It was an ordinary street with double-fronted, brick-veneer houses, neat nature-strips and tidy but uninteresting front gardens. It was a suburb from Melbourne's 60s suburban sprawl which had been left to its own devices as interest moved in subsequent decades back towards the inner city suburbs. It was, I thought, in a way a sister in Melbourne's landscape to the Prahran pool.

The 'party' itself was, unsurprisingly, a pretty dire affair. It resembled a wake, but not a teary emotional wake, rather one of those modern ones that are resolutely cheery and celebratory, even though it's obvious everyone there has cried earlier in the day. It felt manically good natured and extremely tired at the same time.

Mostly it was family. Matt's Mum and Dad were exactly as I'd seen them on tele all those weeks ago, and not, amazingly, a single time since. They were ordinary, conventional people of about 50 a piece, kind, simple, bewildered and obviously sad, but with an abstract confidence about them. I guessed that they were religious and that their faith was, suddenly, horribly, important in a different way than it had ever been before. I couldn't look at them much, and only just managed to be the right side of polite.

Matt's sister, his only sibling, was there. She had also been at the press conference early on. She was solid, in a fit way, and her blonde hair was in a no-nonsense ponytail. She looked as if she played hockey or netball. She had two toddlers with her and they carried on as if everything was fine. At least twice she ate food her kids had tried and didn't like, which seemed vaguely yuk to me, but which she didn't seem to notice let alone mind. She was quiet and obviously concerned for her parents. Her name was Kate. There was no sign of a husband or father.

I didn't recognise anyone else, and mostly forgot their names soon after I was introduced. One of Matt's cousins, a boy of about sixteen was good looking and would be a stunner when he grew up, but as soon as this thought crossed my mind I felt like the biggest old letch in the world and instantly forced it out of my mind.

RT, who went very still and deep-breathing as we arrived, went into meet-and-greet mode as soon as we got inside. He seemed to know virtually everyone and went around them all, giving the men firm handshakes and the women little kisses on the cheek, exchanging words of greeting with all of them. I had never seen him interact with anyone but me and felt proud of him and distanced from him all at the same time.

Nothing, remarkably, was said very much about Matt's disappearance, although everyone spoke about the wonderful things he'd done and said and how great a friend or son or whatever he'd been. The only time the disappearance was mentioned, obliquely, was when an uncle, one of those cheery life-of-the-party dudes who always gives speeches at family gatherings, and was in fact giving a speech, said something about 'when he's back'.

So that was the tack they were taking obviously, heads in the sand and an unshakable belief that Matt would be back and everything would go on as usual. I felt, somehow, as if I myself, who had never even met Matt (well, not properly) knew him better than all these people who were standing around celebrating every little thing he'd ever done. Except maybe for RT. He knew Matt perhaps better than anyone. But he wasn't talking.

After a while I felt stifled. I gently elbowed RT and told him I needed a breath of fresh air, then edged my way out of the room. Everyone was walking around everywhere in the house, so I didn't feel odd doing it, and soon found myself outside in the back garden. It was 8.30

pm by then and just starting to get dark. The backyard was much as you'd expect. There was a thin concrete path, with a slight bend in it halfway, out to a Hills hoist. The fences were lined with neatly edged garden beds with uninteresting plants in them. There was a veggie garden and a couple of fruit trees, aggressively pruned, down the back and a shed in the corner. The expanse of lawn itself was that thick crab-grass, the edges chipped off by the lawn mower and browned here and there. It felt like walking across a mattress.

A woman was standing at the old swing-set, presumably kept for grandkids and younger cousins. It was Matt's sister, and she was having a sneaky cigarette. She nodded at me and gave a little mini-smile like she didn't really give a shit, but didn't mind if I stood with her. I must admit I liked her, jolly-hockey-sticks and all. We reintroduced ourselves and she asked if I'd been a good friend of Matt's. I said that I'd only met him once. Just once, briefly.

'Just once briefly?' she repeated, looking at me as if I might really be a journalist or something.

'I'm actually here with a good friend of his. Gil. You know Gil I think.'

'Oh yeah. Gil.' She continued looking at me slew-eyed. 'You'd think if anyone had any idea …'

I got a bit of a jolt at that. It was the first moment anyone there had acknowledged the disappearance as such, I mean as a big unsolved mystery, rather than just a little hiccup, which would be over when Matt walked back in and picked up his life where he left off.

I asked her what she meant.

'Well he's Matt's best mate, isn't he? Since high school. Kevin was closer for a long time there, but now,' she raised her eyebrows, 'now it seems that went bust about a year ago. But Gil, he's always been right in there. If anyone knows what happened to Matt, it would be him, right. What does he say?'

'I don't ... I don't actually know. I mean, he doesn't talk about it.'

'The police were asking whether he might have gone missing himself. I mean voluntarily disappeared.'

'Why do they say that?'

'They were asking about his peace of mind. The fact that he broke up with Kevin. They seem to think he might have been depressed, you know? What does Gil think? Does he say Matt was depressed or ... or not?'

'He doesn't ... like I say, we don't talk about it.'

She looked at me for a moment then gave me that give-a-shit look again and took a drag on her cigga. She smoked for a bit and looked at the sunset, which wasn't anything special, but was, you know, sunset all the same and something to look at.

'I always thought very highly of him,' she said vaguely after a while. 'Matt. I mean, I loved him of course. But also I thought very highly of him. He'd done so well. He seemed happy with what he had. I mean, the house and Kevin, who I thought was lovely, and he enjoyed his job and seemed ... he just seemed, I suppose, content. I thought they had it great. I thought he was OK. I always thought he'd be OK.'

I nodded, but didn't say anything.

'I don't know, though. I didn't see him all that regularly. He was always good when he was visiting with

99

us. But with three kids, you know, there's a lot going on. Maybe you don't notice straight away. I don't know. Maybe I didn't notice. They asked me, the police, they asked me about his frame of mind. And I had to tell them, I had to say I didn't know, that maybe there was something there, but that I hadn't noticed. And I thought and I thought. And the only thing I can remember is we were talking one day about the kids. I said that before I had the kids I just didn't know what I thought was important, that it felt like everything I did before was nothing, you know, but that at the same time now I often felt like I was being left out somehow. And he sort of scoffed, and said that he felt exactly the same. I don't get that,' she said, and turned from the sunset back to me. 'Do you?'

Maybe somehow, on some level myself personally, I got it, but I didn't have any explanation for her. I shook my head.

I also realised that she had spoken all along about Matt in the past tense.

*

I wonder what Matt's frame of mind was leading up to his disappearance. I mean, I'd wondered so many times what had happened to him, where he'd gone, how he'd left the pool without anyone noticing, why he'd left his stuff, but I'd never really wondered about him and what he might have been feeling the day he disappeared.

On the surface he seemed a regular, almost boringly conventional young man, popular, sociable, fit, healthy, with a good career, a certain amount of financial security, and a generally successful life. His sister thought he had it good. She was proud of him, thought he was 'OK'. And the public, we all thought he had it OK too, didn't we? At first. Perhaps Matt had also felt that his was a successful and happy life. But then, just over the past year or so, he had begun expressing doubts.

Perhaps his life, which had seemed successful, wasn't cutting it any longer. Was he bored with his job, with his home, locked young into a mortgage and a life that he found, a few years into it, that he actually didn't want? That time I met him, briefly, he was talking about that leaf blower, and he looked at me with that wry eyebrow-raised this-is-crap look. OK, I may be remembering more into that small moment than was there, but it fits in with the other things he'd said.

To his sister he'd said that thing about starting to feel 'left behind'. Left behind what or who? Did he mean her? Others? How? Could he have been comparing his life to his sister's and perhaps feeling a sense of disappointment from his family, from society even, from himself, not because he was gay as such, but because that closed off a traditional family, the traditional route, to him? Was he feeling this? Possibly.

Alongside this, of course, there was his relationship with Kevin, which had been degenerating for some time. He no longer felt connected to it, no longer wanted to work it out with counselling and discussion. He was ready to leave and in fact just before his disappearance he did leave.

To RT he'd said he didn't know what he wanted. I think that might be the key to understanding Matt around the time he disappeared. Transition. Maybe knew he didn't want what he had, so let everything wash off him into the pool and was just standing there on the edge, all empty and clean and waiting. I'm sure that's where he was at.

The reality is that I don't know any of this. It could be totally wrong. But maybe I'm right. And if I'm right, does that have anything to do with his disappearance? What did happen to him that day when he disappeared from the pool?

What were the options on that website? Suicide, voluntary disappearance, abduction (murder), abduction (alien) or amnesia.

I don't know about you, but I'm happy to strike alien abduction from the list immediately. No hard feelings Noah. And as for amnesia, I'm not sure how they think that one's going to work either. I mean, even if Matt knocked his head on the edge of the pool doing a tumble turn or something, then wandered away woozily, surely he would have been noticed, especially as he was only wearing Speedos.

Out of the rest, I lean towards voluntary disappearance. That mindset I just described before, don't you think that suggests it? A sense of transition. A new beginning. Maybe Matt wanted to do more than just move out of the Prahran terrace, leave Kevin, separate from his old life. Maybe he wanted to disappear completely and make a super-fresh start. Sure he didn't have to disappear to start fresh. He was financially stable; the sale of the Prahran terrace would have allowed him to have a certain degree of financial security. No incredible debts to run out on, no criminal activity to flee, no shady colleagues to lay low from. None of those reasons for doing it, but remember how he'd spoken to RT that time about swimming laps, and wondered how far he would have got if all his laps were in a straight line? That whole conversation was about escape, I think. About getting out. Maybe he wanted to do it even though he didn't need to?

So where could he have gone? And how did he get there?

As for the first question, he could have gone anywhere. There have been sightings of Matt all over the place, in cities far and wide across Australia. He's a regular featured man, who would normally not stand out in a crowd. Even with the wide circulation of his photo, he would be easy to overlook. Just one more Aussie male in a crowd. Even so, one or more of these sightings could be accurate. He could be anywhere. Sydney. Cairns. Even Apsley. Wherever it is. He could even be there.

As for how, that's a little trickier. Let's just say that he walked away from RT and Paul that day, did his laps, chatted with that blond man at the end of the pool, then simply got out, put his thongs on, which he'd worn to the edge of the pool because he'd known he'd be leaving from there, then walked out, unseen by the girl on the front desk. So far, so easy, but then what? There is no way he could have got far, either on foot, on a tram, or in any way really, without arousing quite a bit of interest. A man walking around the streets, dripping wet in a pair of Speedos would cause some commotion, I'm sure, or at the very least be noticed. And yet no one, not a single person had come forward to report seeing a man in green and white striped Speedos outside the pool that day. No. there's got to be another solution.

The easiest one is that he got into a car out the front of the pool. Not his own, obviously. As we know his car was left at his flat in Hawthorn and his own car keys were left on his keyring in his backpack on the bleachers inside the pool grounds. RT had picked him up and driven him to the pool that day. No, it had to be another car. Someone else's car. Could he have had an accomplice? Someone who met him outside the pool and assisted him in his disappearance. Kevin? No, Kevin was too straight to have conspired in Matt's disappearance. Kate? Bullshit. His family obviously weren't the type who would do that sort of stuff.

Which leaves RT. You know, I can imagine RT helping Matt out. He was probably Matt's closest friend, someone he confided in. If Matt had decided on a voluntary disappearance and wanted someone to talk it over with, to help plan the details and perhaps even help him on the day, I can imagine RT doing all that without a qualm. Or can I? I'm not sure.

So how did they work it? That day at the pool? The simplest way would have been for RT to give his car keys to Matt when they arrived at the pool, then Matt could simply have walked out of the pool after his laps, taken the car, which was parked directly out the front of the pool and driven off. There could have been a change of clothes in the boot. And then he simply drove away.

Where to? Somewhere in Melbourne? A flat or another property he had arranged, on the sly, in another suburb? Or perhaps he had driven to the airport and from there gone much further away? If he flew anywhere, he obviously didn't fly under his own name or it would have been picked up. But he could have flown under someone else's name. Not I suppose a terribly hard thing to do, especially not if you were able to steal someone's wallet, and book a ticket in their name, using their license for identity purposes. It wouldn't be difficult if you chose someone who looked like you, say at the pool, then lifted their wallet from their bag while they were swimming. It could be done, I suppose.

Before the police even got to the pool that day Matt could have been at the airport, and maybe at the airport, just before he boarded whatever plane he was going to get on, maybe he called RT's mobile and told him all had gone OK, told him where the car was left in the airport car park, which level and which location, and that the car keys were, perhaps, on the top of the back tyre, and the next day RT could have taken the bus out to the airport and retrieved his car, with no one the wiser.

The police, of course, hadn't checked RT's belongings on that day to see if his car keys were there, they didn't check to see his car was out the front and whether he left the pool that night by car or by public transport, and if they checked the call history of his mobile phone, which they must have done, we never heard about it. Negative evidence, all of it, I know, but still it could be significant.

Even as I was imagining all this I didn't believe it. Mainly because of two things: the sale of the Prahran terrace and Matt's Hawthorn flat.

Surely if Matt was planning to disappear and start a new life somewhere else it seems incredible that he would do so before the sale of his Prahran house and the financial settlement between himself and Kevin. OK, so perhaps he didn't care about that. Perhaps he was salting money away into a different account all year, or even just building up a stash of cash to run away with. Who knows? But still, I feel sure he wouldn't have just walked out mere weeks before settlement on the sale of the Prahran terrace.

And what about the flat in Hawthorn? Would you move into a flat and presumably pay a month of bond and a month of rent, when you were planning to cut loose, disappear and start afresh somewhere else? I can't imagine why he would have done that.

However, the main thing that makes me wonder about the whole voluntary disappearance solution is the way he disappeared. I mean, why would he do it like that, from the pool, dripping wet, in Speedos, when he could quite easily have done it, to the same effect, either with or without RT's help and RT's car, at any other time? I just can't believe anyone would choose to disappear like that.

*

When I went back inside, RT grabbed my hand and hoiked his head slightly to the side, indicating the door. I turned and walked back out into the entry hall. Red Trunks followed me then further indicated that we should go upstairs.

I asked if he was sure and he said they wouldn't mind so we went up the stairs. They were shallow steps and steep and the stairs curved back on themselves so that when I went up a few steps after Red Trunks, I found my face virtually right in his bum. I had a flashback to nosing in his crack like a vacuum cleaner which felt perfectly inappropriate in the current setting, like ogling Matt's sixteen-year-old cousin, so I put it out of my mind. When we emerged upstairs the ceiling seemed subtly a little bit lower, and this along with the shrunken, pokey stairs made it feel like we'd grown slightly bigger on the trip upstairs, like Alice who'd eaten something that says 'Eat me'.

Along the passageway there were a number of doors. Red Trunks lead the way and I followed close behind. Our feet made no noise on the carpet and none of the doors made any noise as Red Trunks opened them. First there was a bathroom, clean and cool. Then a bedroom on the other side of the passageway. Obviously it faced the sun and the curtains had been carefully shut to try and keep the room cool. It hadn't worked. It was dim and stuffy like dusty carpet and stale scent. There was a double bed with a couple of items of clothing strewn over it. Obviously the master bedroom occupied by Matt's parents. Next door along, another bedroom, this one with a single bed and a suitcase sitting beside it. Lastly, at the end of the passageway, was a third bedroom and this one I knew as soon as Red Trunks opened the door and I got a peek over his shoulder, was the one he was heading for. It seemed small, like a child's bedroom. A single bed. A built-in robe. A small desk, with a map of the globe inlaid in the top. A lamp. A shelf with trophies on it. Books. Magazines. Marks where posters had been taken off the wall. This had, I knew, been Matt Gray's bedroom when he lived at home.

I asked Red Trunks if he'd been in there before. He nodded, looked at me briefly, then back at the bed.

He told me how he and Matt would hang out in there sometimes after school. How they'd bring stuff up there to eat and read magazines or listen to music. He pointed to where there was the mark of a poster having been taken down off the wall and said, 'I think that was a Ferrari poster. Or Blondie maybe.'

I could imagine it just as he said. Two teenage boys, the usual, the totally typical adolescent bedroom, the same conversations, the same slightly putrid adolescent smell which wasn't a million miles away from the sex-stench of Sharon's Place after me and RT were done with it.

I stepped further into the room and opened one of the cupboard doors. It was empty but there was *Star Wars* wallpaper on the walls inside, from a time even further back when Matt had been a child in the 70s.

Behind me Red Trunks sat down on the single bed with his hands between his knees and a scowling squint on his face which obviously meant he was trying to hold in check some emotion or other. He was finding it tough to be there, obviously, and yet he seemed determined. He must have had his own thing going on about Matt, and sure it would be very confusing to have one of your best mates just disappear on you like that, but this place was creeping me out too. I mean in a different way. Matt Gray couldn't have lived there beyond high school. He had a partner and a mortgage in his early 20s for Christ's sake, so he must have moved out way back then. That meant he hadn't lived in that room for at least fifteen years or something. More like twenty. And yet it looked just like a teenager's bedroom. Why had his parents kept that bedroom exactly like it must have been the last time Matt lived with them? Being in that bedroom made it feel like Matt Gray had disappeared twenty years rather than twenty days ago.

Poor Red Trunks looked so big and clumsy jack-knifed into the middle of the single bed. I went over, sat next to him and put my arm across his shoulders. He was too big to comfort like that—it felt stupid, but what do you do?

'Where is he?'

He asked it like it was a quiz question in the Sunday lift-out or something. Sort of pondering it, but not seriously, as if he knew the answers were printed in very small and upside-down text some odd pages further on.

He picked up a couple of things, a little gecko made of lime green material and stuffed with sand, a pen from the Big Pineapple, then put them back exactly where they had been and stared at the wall.

'I just wish I hadn't ... I wish it'd been ...'

He didn't finish. Whatever he was going to say, whatever regret he was going to express, didn't come out. So I told him not to think about it. (Of course. What else would I say?) I patted his shoulder and planted a little kiss on his ear which was the only bit of his face I could reach. He was hot and clammy and seemed all screwed up tight, and I suddenly felt like I had earlier, downstairs; close to him but at the same time distant, and panicked because I didn't know him. It was odd, because the way we'd been seeing each other it didn't matter what we knew about each other, in fact it was great that we knew nothing, it was all about sex and the here-and-now, but there in that freaked-out bedroom it mattered because I'd seen something of the real RT. He'd brought me with him and if not precisely shared what he was feeling with me, then at least allowed me to be there with him in that room and see him feel it. I wanted to comfort him, but I couldn't really comfort him, not really, because I had no clue what he was like and what he was feeling. And my panic, I guess, came from thinking, Here's someone who's worth knowing and you don't know him, here's someone who needs something from you and you can't give it to him. And in my head I was saying to myself, quite harshly, What are you doing? What are you doing with yourself? What are you doing here? What are you doing?

I stood up abruptly. So did RT. Suddenly the little bedroom seemed too full of gay men. I said that I thought we should go. He agreed.

*

That night RT and I had sex almost as soon as we got back to Sharon's Place. It was intense and serious and RT was throwing us around a bit, rolling all over Mr T's big beige bed, with the sheets and eventually all four pillows on the floor. With the sliding doors closed to the hot night and the curtains closed to the starlight the room was dim and soon became fusty and airless. I felt for a second in there somewhere completely overwhelmed and a little scared. But then I realised that I was not the only one who believed in sugar pill sex and that perhaps because of my inability to comfort RT earlier in the evening I owed him a rough fuck. I felt good that at least there was something I could do for him, but at the same time I felt like a whore because that was all I could do.

*

I never did learn to speak Spanish.

In the months just before going to Spain, Leo sent me a Spanish phrase book. More than that, he sent me his own tongue-in-cheek, hand-written lessons on how to speak Spanish phonetically. They were illustrated with either cute little stick-figure-style illustrations, or pictures cut out of magazines. I got a laugh out of the phrases he was sending me to learn, but I never bothered actually learning any. I mean, what's the point of learning how to say, 'The birds, they scare me!' in Spanish just because we'd watched Hitchcock's *The Birds* together and enjoyed it?

So when I first got to Spain I couldn't speak a word of Spanish, couldn't understand a thing. I ended up learning a few, a very few, words. Of course the first of them was hello, *Hola*. I must admit I ended up saying *hola* for everything. It became like some generic expression which could mean anything. Like, when we were walking down a particularly skinny alleyway and a car swept past and its mirror actually knocked me on the wrist, I said *Hola!* in a tone as if to say, 'Hey! Watch it!' Another time when Leo and I were busy at it in some hotel somewhere and Housekeeping knocked on the door and started opening it, I called *Hola!* from the bed as if to say, 'Ooo. Hang on. We're in here!' And if we were out at a nightclub or something, and dancing and drinking and just generally whooping it up, *Hola!* became a general 'woo hoo', like *Ole!* or something. You know? It was the only Spanish word I ever used. No, that's not quite true. I could also order a gin and tonic in Spanish which is basically just *Dos ginebra et tonica, por favor.*

The G&Ts in Spain were incredible. They didn't measure the gin quite as anally as I was used to in Australia. None of those little boxy measuring-cup spout things on the bottle. They just slopped the gin in quite generously over the ice and topped up with a splash of tonic. After about three I was nearly on the floor.

It was that night, the night I learnt how to order a gin and tonic, that I met a girl called, I think, Esther. Leo and I were at some club in central Barcelona. It was packed and the music was loud and I was pretty pissed but having a wonderful time. Esther was beautiful in a cliched Spanish way, with dark eyes and hair and a sense of sexual threat about her. God knows how old she was, maybe only a teenager. All the teens in Spain looked confident and sexual, but then again they also seemed to hag out really early.

Esther was wearing braces I remember, over a teeshirt this is, not on her teeth, and also had her wrist wrapped in bandages. She pointed to her wrist, then leant in and started talking to me. Of course the music was really loud and we were right in front of a speaker so I couldn't hear a word she said, and of course since she was speaking in Spanish it didn't matter anyhow. I squinted and watched her lips, which made no difference but seemed somehow the polite thing to do, you know? Then I shrugged my shoulders, spread my hands, shook my head and made a face that said, 'Can't hear—don't understand.' And so she did this mime for me, a quite intricate mime about how she was riding on something, a bike or something, and that something, a car I presumed, but of course it could have been a dog or anything really, came out from a side street and that she had swerved to avoid it and crashed into a parked car, somersaulted over the handlebars and landed on the road, spraining her wrist.

Through the whole performance she was talking as well, describing what she was performing in words, and towards the end a word popped out at me that I heard over the music and understood.

'Vespa?' I asked. Then shouted again, 'Vespa?'

And she nodded and smiled and shouted back, 'Vespa! Si Vespa!'

We cheered each other and hugged and kept nodding and congratulating each other on our mutual understanding. I can't believe how excited we seemed to be about it. Personally, I felt like I cracked some code or learnt the entire Spanish language, or something; although yes, I am aware that 'Vespa' isn't exactly a Spanish word, but who cares? And apparently Esther felt the same. We danced and drank the rest of the night through, buoyed by our happy little communication, which by the way, we didn't attempt again all night.

Other than those few pathetic examples, I was totally unable to communicate with anyone in Spain aside from Leo, other than a few shopkeepers here and there. Leo was the only one in Spain I knew who spoke English, and yet I felt like I communicated in mime with gorgeous Esther with the broken wrist better than I was able to in my mother tongue with Leo, with Leo and RT together.

*

RT was a mystery to me. I mean, a total mystery. Obviously he cared about Matt. Obviously. But other than that, who knew? He had his own thing going on inside that head of his, he must have, and it must have hurt, or maybe just confused him. But I didn't know what it was all about. He didn't talk to me about those sorts of things. About Matt or me or anything. He was the real strong and silent type we all dream about, but I tell you it's not romantic at all, it's just fucking annoying.

I mean, bit by bit, I pieced things together. He would let bits slip, about how he felt about the disappearance, how it was affecting him, what Matt had been like; but it was hard work, kind of like being on an archaeological dig, and I was there fwisking sand around with a little toothbrush, and every now and then I'd find a dino femur or something and put it away with a whole lot of other bones to look at later and maybe put together.

That's what conversation with RT was like. He would talk, every now and then about Matt. Like he'd answer a question before thinking, and then some information was out there before he closed down on the subject. And later, another day, there'd be another bit of information. He would seem to not want to talk about it or think about it, in fact he'd said exactly that to me, and yet the next moment he would take me with him to see Matt's bedroom. He was showing me bits and pieces, and then hiding them again. And so, even though I'd pieced together bits of information about RT and Matt, and stuff surrounding the disappearance, it still felt unclear and unfinished. There were bits of femur in there, but the whole skeletal structure was still unclear.

I asked RT one day whether he'd had a crush on Matt. He nodded, quite simply, and said, 'Back in high school.' That was it. No more conversation around it. But it made me remember my own high school crushes on boys and I thought, well it can't be very different. I had a crush on a boy called Shane at school. Real bogan type. I used to go and watch him play basketball and sit on the side-lines minding his bag and his tracksuit top or whatever, barracking and feeling proud. I mean, I didn't know enough to label myself gay at that stage, I just thought Shane was great and that lots of boys felt like this about other boys. I didn't want to kiss him or touch his dick or anything like that. I wasn't very sexual at that stage. But I remember being squished in the back of his Mum's car with these other boys on the basketball team on the way to some game or something, and me and Shane were scrunched up together in the back seat, touching all along our sides. I got hot, and my skin was all buzzy and I loved it but still didn't process that feeling. Maybe that was RT and Matt.

So what happened with that crush? Well, if I have to guess, and I suppose I do because it's unlikely RT will ever tell me, exactly nothing happened to it. I mean, think about how reserved and silent RT was, then imagine it with awkward adolescence spread over it. He would probably have tortured himself thinking of all these conversations that might happen, or all those soft-focus little moments that might happen, and trying to get up the courage to instigate something, anything, but never doing a single thing.

So RT, reticent and stolid even in adolescence, wasn't able to tell Matt how he felt about him. And Matt? What was he doing all this time? Apparently, so RT said in another unguarded moment, Matt had gone through a string of girlfriends during high school, but RT thought they were probably doing nothing much but 'a bit of fingering and dry-humping.'

Then along came University and Kevin. Kevin would have been a couple of years older, and probably a lot more articulate than RT, and he and Matt got together and got themselves a mortgage and an inner-suburban life, and that was that.

In the years to follow, RT's silly school-days crush would turn into genuine and very deep friendship. Maybe for RT it became, 'I *used to* have a crush on Matt.' And maybe he believed it. Maybe it was true. But when it started going badly between Matt and Kevin, things may have changed. Suddenly Matt would be wanting to spend more time out of the house, away from Kevin. He would call RT more, meet up with him more, stay out a bit later so he, Matt, didn't have to go home to the terrace. They'd talk more over Matt's situation, his difficulties, his problems, 'the situation'. Matt would need RT more and pay more attention to him. And it could feel, couldn't it, a bit like the old buzz?

Maybe all those years it was like RT had been thinking subconsciously, If only Kevin hadn't come along we'd be together, or, if only Matt would leave Kevin we could get it together. Maybe Kevin became, in RT's head 'the reason', and so the moment the Kevin-plug was pulled, all this stuff came gooshing out of him, some perfectly formed scenario in his head, like some girl who's dreamt of her wedding day since she was six years old. RT and Matt, together. All Disney and happily ever after. But it didn't happen like that. We know that. For whatever reason it didn't happen. Had there been a scene? Had RT (and he would, of course, never be capable of talking about something like this) 'tried it on'? Was there a moment when Matt was crying on RT's shoulder, either literally or not, and where finally, after all these years, after the Kevin bath-plug had been pulled, he finally said something or did something? Put his hand on Matt somewhere, on his leg or his shoulder, and let it linger a little longer or squeeze in a way that meant, This is different—do you get it? Did he try to kiss him or hug him, maybe, all awkward and big and burly? Or did he tell him, just say something to him. Maybe simply, 'What about us?' Maybe with a laugh, pretending it's a joke until he knows Matt's reaction, with that constipated concentrating frown on his forehead. Maybe in the car, staring fixedly ahead at the road, or at his place, where I had never been, on the couch with a DVD on or something. I don't know. And Matt? What did Matt say? Maybe he didn't say anything. Maybe his eyes re-focussed and his thoughts shifted from his own preoccupations and he looked at RT and realised what was going on and just thought, 'Oh shit.'

Of course all this was only in my imagination. I knew none of it other than the bits of information I was able to glean from RT. But if he wouldn't tell me I had to make it up, you know what I mean?

8

One day somewhere around then Noah was arrested. It was the head story on the late news one night, but they'd obviously rushed to get it on because it only had the absolute basics, just that the police had charged Noah with obstructing a police enquiry. They showed archive stuff of Noah, and a quick shot of him leaving the police station, but there was no new footage.

First thing the next morning I left RT sleeping soundly and went out for the papers (stuff him and his conversations with the supermarket woman) and a large coffee. I was looking forward to the papers that morning, and wasn't disappointed. The headline was simply, LIAR, with the photo of the recently over-exposed hamburger cheeks of Noah, photographed in paparazzi style exiting the St Kilda Road police headquarters with his hand imperfectly hiding his face from the click click flash flash of the camera.

It seemed that the police became suspicious about Noah due to the precise mixture of clothing, all allegedly belonging to Matt, found in his, Noah's, apartment. The clothing was completely listed in the article that morning and I read it, not getting it, but knowing that it would be explained. There was a pair of swimwear, not the green and white striped swimmers Matt was wearing on the day he disappeared, but a light blue pair, quite old, with stretched elastic. There was a white Bonds teeshirt, plus another teeshirt with a Nike logo on it. There was also a large range of underwear and other sports wear including running shorts and singlets and lycra bike shorts. And then there was a pair of white plastic thongs, that same pair of white thongs that Noah had been photographed with after the charred body had been found in the warehouse in Kensington.

When Noah originally came forward the police, faced pretty much with a blank wall in the disappearance case, were eager to investigate Noah's connection with Matt, and investigated the premise that Matt could have walked from the pool to Noah's apartment, which was literally just around the corner. Given that he had disappeared from the pool wearing only his green and white striped togs, this seemed like it might be the first positive break they'd got.

In order to confirm Noah's story, the police asked Kevin to identify the clothing as belonging to Matt if he could. The light blue swimwear Kevin identified as probably belonging to Matt, as well as various items of underwear that he said were the same size and brand that Matt wore, but that as there were no specific identifying marks in them he couldn't of course be positive that they in fact did belong to Matt. (I must admit I sniggered a bit at the thought of 'identifying marks' in underwear. I didn't personally think a skid-mark would hold up in court, but who am I to say?)

Kevin also said that Matt had a Nike shirt which was, if not this exact one, then one exactly like it. As for the rest of the clothing, it all seemed relatively new and Kevin apparently said it could therefore have been purchased by

119

Matt after he had moved out. Yes, Matt had been in the habit of wearing those types of sports things. The thongs? They were also new, but of the right brand and size.

The police accepted that the clothes belonged to Matt and went on with their investigations. However, after a week to think it over, Kevin came back to the police saying he had remembered that one of Matt's teeshirts found in Noah's apartment, the one with the Nike logo on it, had been stolen months before Matt had disappeared.

Apparently earlier in the year, when Matt was still living with Kevin, their clothes dryer had broken down and during an especially rainy week Matt had taken two loads of washing to a close-by laundromat to dry them. Later, at home, Kevin and Matt discovered that a number of their clothes from that wash had disappeared and they suspected they had been stolen from the dryer at the laundromat, during a ten minute window when Matt left the premises to go to the corner shop for a newspaper. Matt had told Kevin at the time that there was another person in the laundromat who was gone when he returned with his newspaper. They suspected that this person had stolen the clothes, but short of the fact that it was a man, Matt didn't remember anything else about him. They had not reported it to the police at the time. Matt's new Nike teeshirt was amongst the clothes stolen and, although Kevin couldn't be sure, he thought some of the underwear found at Noah's flat was also amongst the clothes taken that day.

After this evidence that some, if not all, of the clothes in Noah's apartment had probably been stolen, some long before Matt had disappeared, and that a number of the remaining items had obviously been purchased relatively recently, the police, after expert advice (what sort of expert they did not explain) came to the conclusion that what they were looking at in this collection of clothing was not the normal remnants that someone might leave at a partner's apartment, but a collection of fetish wear. In short they suspected that the clothes had either been stolen from Matt or purchased new by Noah himself.

From here the police spokesperson unemotionally but somewhat ominously stated that they had 'a further interview' with Noah and that he admitted outright that he had lied, that the clothes were not left in his flat by Matt, that Matt had never even been to his flat and that he, Noah, had in fact never met or spoken to Matt at any time.

There was no direct comment from Noah, who had declined to speak to the journalist, and absolutely no mention of UFOs anywhere in the article at all. However, if the past fortnight was anything to go by, Noah would even now be selling his story to the highest bidder. I had no doubt there wouldn't be long to wait before I saw his slab-face in the newspapers again.

*

The next day there were a couple of young show-ponies at the pool whom I just adored, a couple of young boys, surely no older than 18, who had decided to dress up for the occasion. They were skinny, pale little whippets of things, with badly dyed hatchet jobs for hairdos, one with a very white-blond fringe. They wore matching huge bug-eyed sunglasses, matching yellow shorts with white polka-dots, and each had a yellow blow-up ring. They tittered down to the edge of the pool, wearing the blow-up rings around their hips like tutus, then climbed awkwardly down the steps into the water, helping each other to squeeze their plastic rings through the handrails, with of course lots of amusing and inappropriate squeaking sounds, which they laughed like drains at. After this little performance, and with all eyes definitely on them, they stood in the water talking for a while, pretending to be blase about the attention but not at all convincingly. Then, after only a few minutes they made another big production out of getting out of the pool and came back to their towels. They looked quite pleased with themselves.

Some wag just down from me said in an aside to I don't know who, 'Get back in the closet, kids, you're not done yet.' But I didn't think that was very generous. I liked that they were having a bit of campy fun with it. It reminded me of my own club-kid youth, when the biggest thing about going out anywhere was what you were going to wear, the sillier the better. I had gone on and on with this dress-up aesthetic all through my early twenties until one day I got off a bus and saw myself in a shop window and thought, 'you look like a fuckwit,' right out of the blue, just like that. Really harsh, but that's how it was. I suddenly felt like a total dickhead and from that moment stopped dying my hair odd colours and wearing my weird-ass collection of second-hand clothes. Although I did relive the magic every now and then for special occasions. But not for many years now. When one hits 30, I think the time has come to leave dress-ups for the kids.

Oh God, that just makes me remember something else. My sister and I had a 'dress-up box' when we were kids, which had heaps of Mum and Dad's old clothes in there. There were plenty of bizarre little numbers from the early 70s, but I remember I was mostly fascinated by a floor length peach nightdress which had a split up each leg, right up to the hip. I can't imagine my mother ever wearing that. Well, actually I guess I can, she was a bit va-va-voom back in 1972, but I can't imagine her wearing it for my father's appreciation. And yes I did wear it. I even remember getting together with some other poof-in-training called Rickie at primary school and doing a dress-up show at school. God knows why the teachers let us, and God knows how I was confident enough to do something like that, but when you're a kid you don't get those boundaries or those fears. If you like putting on one of your Mum's old nighties at home, then why not do it for assembly in front of the entire school? The school must have called my parents, though, because soon after that the dress-up box, including that incredible peach negligee nightie thing, went missing. I asked Mum where the dress-up box had gone and she said quite calmly that she'd burnt it. We had a little incinerator out in the backyard for garden rubbish and stuff, and so they burnt it. This reaction might seem a little extreme, but I remember thinking nothing of it at the time—they were always burning things, my parents. They had this country kind of slash-and-burn thing going on, where if you didn't use something almost daily, you should get rid of it. In the years since I've left home, I can remember heaps of phone calls with my Mum where in the middle of the conversation she'll suddenly say something like, 'Oh, you know all those drawings of yours under your bed at home, you didn't want those did you?' I'd ask suspiciously, 'Why?' And Mum would say, 'Because we burnt them.' You go to their house these days and think, Where's all their stuff? There's virtually no furniture there. Just the absolute essentials. My parents are pyromaniacs.

I ended up getting together with Rickie years later in high school when we were in the chorus of the school production of *Camelot* together, both wearing tights and so at the peak of adolescent horniness we stunk of it. He asked me about the peach negligee and I had to tell him about the incinerator. He also seemed a bit disappointed. If I had it now, I think I'd frame it.

Anyhow, I liked those little lemon-yellow boys at the pool. Good luck to them. They should enjoy their dressing up as much as they can before they get to their very own 'you look like a fuckwit' moment. If they do. I suppose not everyone does.

*

After the *LIAR* article and accompanying paparazzi shot, which augured well for future instalments of his story, Noah went to ground and didn't say a word. He left his public, previously studiously courted, completely starved for more information about why he had lied to police, to the whole city, to the world. Perhaps our interest was especially piqued, at least I know mine was, by that brilliant throw-away description of the clothes Noah claimed belonged to Matt being in reality 'a collection of fetish wear'.

I was just admiring Noah's apparent restraint when he made his move. Rumour had it that his full and detailed 'confession' would be in the next edition of one of Australia's trashiest weekly magazines. I, for one, couldn't wait. But, amazingly, sadly, ironically, and above all fucking-hilariously, Noah's full and detailed 'confession' never made it into print. He never got the glossy cover he seemed to covet, for just days before the Noah edition was due to hit the stands, Anna Nicole Smith died and every cover of every trashy tabloid magazine the world over that could be scrapped was scrapped.

So that's how it all played out. Noah's last big hurrah was harrumphed by the larger than life and now dead Texan waitress. If it wasn't bad enough being bumped from one edition, he didn't even make it into the next one. In the cruel world of the tabloids, last week's front cover was this week's recycling. A 9-day wonder didn't even seem to last 9 days any longer. Noah, I felt sure, would have been livid.

Even though it never saw the light of day, I was able to find on the internet a full transcript of the interview, which I'm sure was more interesting than the eventual article would have turned out to be. In the transcript as it existed online there was no editing, no paraphrasing, no journalistic jingoism, nothing to get in the way of what Noah was saying. And he certainly said a lot. I guessed that Noah had decided to put everything into this last throw of the dice, and for once the trash-mag hyperbole was right and this actually could have turned out to be his real, full story, or 'confession'.

Noah began by detailing his childhood. It was predictably shabby. His father had left. His mother was on welfare. He lived, in fact, in one of those council hi-rise apartment blocks of the same type that overshadowed the Prahran pool, although he had lived in the block in Collingwood. His childhood had been unremarkable, except for a very little trouble with the police for shoplifting. He was, he said, a very reserved and quiet young boy who struggled with school and with making friends. He was also, he discovered from a fairly early age, gay.

'I was so quiet. So reserved and withdrawn. I was unable to meet other gay men. I tried the classifieds, and that was OK for a while, but the few men I met up with, well, they weren't often what they said they were, and anyhow they rejected me pretty quickly. I was no good socially and of course I don't look like they want a boyfriend to look, do I? No one would look at me or talk to me. I just felt invisible you know? I got to the point where I just thought, Why bother. What's the point? I just felt like I wasn't ever going to meet anybody, you know? It was hopeless and I felt pretty down about myself. So I just gave up.

The journo asked a question then about Matt. About where he came into it.

'I just saw him one day walking down my street, in front of my flats I mean, and I remember thinking when I saw him, He's just a normal, everyday, nice-looking kind of guy, and I wanted a boyfriend just like that, but at the same time I sort of wanted to be like that myself. If that makes sense.

'Anyhow, I kept seeing him around. He would regularly walk past my place, with a backpack on, I suppose going to the pool to do his laps, or coming home afterwards. One time I saw him walk past and I just decided to follow him. So yeah, I ended up following him quite a bit. I followed him to his house, so knew where he lived. It was only a short walk from my place. I didn't feel like I was doing anything wrong, but I suppose I was. Invading his privacy and all that. But it didn't feel like that. I mean, I had no intention of doing anything to him. I just wanted to watch him.'

The journalist then said, 'But you didn't just watch him did you?'

'No. No, that's true. I didn't … I started taking things as well. His clothes mainly. I took things from his clothes line a couple of times. Underwear, and a pair of his swimming togs. I also took some of his things from a dryer one time down at the laundromat. I took a few other things from their yard, silly things like a hoe they left in the garden and a boot-scraper from their front porch. I mean, I couldn't do a thing with those and just left them in the park near my place. I also took their mail once. But there was nothing in it except bills and stuff, so I chucked it out.

'I mean, the truth is, I suppose … well, I became obsessed with him, didn't I? I didn't have much of a life of my own. I came to feel as if I knew him, like we had things in common. I even felt that he knew I was following him and didn't mind, and that sometimes, even, he was following me as well. Seriously. I was convinced he was following me sometimes. I could feel it. But whenever I turned around, he was never there. I would tell myself that he could have just slipped behind a tree. I convinced myself that he was there. There was more. I would think of conversations we had, might have, together. And things we might do together. And they became like real memories not made up ones.

'I was convinced, believe it or not, that I was also having a sexual relationship with him. I know that sounds odd. I mean, at first, yeah, sure, I used to masturbate while thinking about him and just imagine having sex with him. Sometimes I would wear his things. Sometimes I would just look at them. Or maybe leave them around my room, like he'd been there and just left them on the floor or over the back of a chair. But then, when I started to think that he was following me, I also thought he was sneaking into my flat at night, while I was asleep, coming into my bedroom and slipping his hands under the sheets and touching me. And I would wake up, you know, hard and half asleep and I'd be convinced that he'd just slipped out. I would do things like leave my bedroom window open so he could get in easily. I mean, I knew it wasn't really happening, but at the same time I believed it was.'

'What about the disappearance?' the Journo then asked. 'Tell me what happened there.'

'Well, I had nothing to do with that. I swear. Nothing. I mean, I knew about that the same time everyone else did, when it was in the papers. At first I was kind of confused and angry about it, I suppose. I found it hard to believe it had happened, because I hadn't imagined it. You know? But then after a few days I sort of just processed it into my memories with everything else and it seemed like the rest. You know, real. And that's when I went to the police. I never ever meant to upset or mislead anyone. I honestly believed it was true. But then again, as soon as the police told me they thought I was making it all up I knew that was true too, so I just admitted it.

The journalist again, pushing, 'So you never actually spoke to, had any contact with Matt? Nothing whatsoever?'

'The truth is I never even spoke to Matt. Not once. I heard him talking on the mobile one time, quite early on this was, but that was it. I don't know who he was talking to, but he was telling them he didn't want to go somewhere, I think it was to some event or some party or dinner or something. And as he was explaining himself I sort of felt I understood something about him. I was sure I did. I knew that he was sick of his life and wanted something else, someone else. It was in the way he stood, the tone of voice, everything. I just knew it. But you see, that's the thing, I don't actually know anything about him, not really, do I? It's all just in my imagination. That's what I have to come to terms with.'

It was pretty full-on stuff as far as confessions went. And sad. I'd expected to laugh out loud, but didn't. I was, I admit, just starting to feel a little like the poor unfortunate mixed-up kid had been taken advantage of by the trashy tabloid journalist and through association by us all. However, from then on the journo who to this point had been pretty hard line switched tack and tell-all became forgive-all.

There were, it transpired, actually no formal charges laid against Noah. He was also in counselling for his delusional behaviour and had actually, through all his media activity over the last couple of weeks, met a man that he had started seeing. It seemed too quick a recovery to me, but after the story he'd just told I felt inclined to overlook this.

There were of course a few things to tidy up. One of them was a word or two about the whole UFO thing. Here Noah must have sounded amused, and he admitted that he did in fact believe in UFOs, but didn't believe that aliens had abducted Matt Gray.

'What do you think I am? An idiot?'

Then what did he think had happened to Matt Gray? Noah said he didn't know, but that he hoped for the sake of Matt's family, and all Matt's friends, 'his real friends', that he would be found soon.

I'd always had a bit of a soft spot for Noah. He seemed such a funny and melodramatic little Muppet, saying such strange and provocative things, gazing up into the sky mysteriously or earnestly clutching those white thongs, the ones he'd obviously purchased earlier that day especially for the photo-shoot.

And of course, now that I knew Noah had his own fleeting 'leaf-blower' moment with Matt, overhearing him on the mobile phone that time, I felt, I must admit, a bit of a twinge of sisterhood. I thought to myself, I hope he's going to be OK. You know? He's the type that so easily might not be.

*

It was the day after I read the tell-all Noah story that everything went a bit pear-shaped. The weather had been overcast for a couple of days, so I hadn't been to the pool. Instead I'd spent time with RT at Sharon's Place. The tone ever since the visit to Matt's parents' place and the little scene in Matt's old bedroom was kind of like the weather, overcast and shit. We still had sex a lot, but it didn't seem the same, well not for me.

Anyhow, a few nights after the visit to Matt's parents' place, we were chop-sticking noodles into our gobs, and about 45 minutes into *Sliver*, which we were watching as part of a Sharon Stone movie marathon in honour of Mr T's pad, it all blew up.

I asked, out of the blue during a toilet break, whether he thought Matt's family really believed that Matt would come back. And then RT just went off. Just went right off. He threw the noodles back down on the table, but they went off the edge and all over the carpet and we stared at them for a second all wide-eyed as if they were blood or something. Then he asked me why I kept asking about Matt. He repeated it a few times, like, Why, why, why are you doing that? It was kind of like the outburst about the questionnaires in the papers and the graphs and stuff, except this time it was directed at me. I felt horrible about upsetting him, of course, but really I was feeling more wary, I guess, wary of this side of RT that was all bottled up and came bursting out like this.

Of course I apologised. I said that I was sorry and that I didn't realise it was upsetting him so much. He just scowled at the tele at Shazza and the Baldwin guy on pause, and then said after a minute or two that it was difficult for him. Then he started crying and it was like Matt's bedroom all over again and I was putting my arm across his shoulders, although it seemed physically awkward, and saying things that I don't remember, but which were, you know, vaguely comforting, like he was a horse spooked by a car.

Something was tearing him up about Matt, something more than the simple fact that he was missing. What was it? That he loved Matt? I mean, obviously he did, that was easy to see. But it didn't seem that simple even. There was guilt there, somewhere, about something. It was only guilt that could rip you up quite like that. Did he know something about what happened to Matt? Did he, after all, have something to do with it?

'What happened with Matt?' I asked.

He looked at me. His eyes were all glassy from crying, but I saw in them something different, something that I'd never seen there before. It was something unsure and vulnerable. It was fear. He was scared. But scared of what? Of me it seemed. But what could I do to him? Why on earth would he be scared of me? Then I realised. He was scared because he was contemplating finally letting everything out. He was afraid of me because he was going to tell me the truth.

'Tell me,' I said. 'Tell me what happened.'

'I … I picked him up. And … and took him to the pool,' he said.

OK. He picked Matt up and took him to the pool that day. We knew that. So?

He was still looking at me with those misty eyes, but there was something else in there. Not just fear, but also that trusting look you sometimes get from a lover that says, 'OK, I'm going to get one of those things, one of those chest-saw tools from the coroner's office and I'm going to crack through my ribs and open them up like cupboard doors and scoop out my insides and give them to you to look after. Will you be OK with that?'

I know that feeling. I know that look.

Anyhow, I pretty much said to RT, 'Yes, sure, give me your insides and I'll pass them gently through my hands and wash them with warm soapy water and then put them back in for you.'

And he did. Talk I mean. And when he decided to start it all came out in one big gush. I was just the emetic.

'He called me,' RT said. 'The morning he disappeared. He said please could I come and get him. Take him out somewhere. He suggested the pool. He sounded really down. He sounded, different. I said ... I started saying something ... and he said to me, and his voice went lower, he said, 'Please. Please do this.' And it was horrible to hear him say it like that. It was horrible. Of course I went over. I went to his flat in Hawthorn. I'd never been there before. It was half empty and the curtains were pulled shut. Matt was there. He seemed OK. A bit flat, but OK. And he put his hand on my arm and said, 'Thanks for this,' in that same flat voice. But on the way, in the car on the way, he said, he wondered whether he'd done the right thing or whether he'd made a horrible mistake. And then he shook his head and said, 'I don't have a clue what I'm doing.' His face was just so pale, his voice was so flat and his eyes were all wired. I wondered if he was on something. He might have been. I thought, Oh shit, he's going to do something silly.'

'Something silly? Like harm himself?'

'I don't know,' RT said and his eyes went all glassy again. 'I just don't know what happened to him.' He shook his head, all bewildered and hurt and guilty. Yes guilty.

'I don't know,' he said. 'And I should.'

We didn't finish watching *Sliver*. We turned the DVD
and the tele off, went to bed and just lay in each other's
arms for a bit. After a while RT's voice came out of the
darkness. He thanked me. I said 'no problem', but in
actual fact I was wondering what the fuck I was going to
do with his intestines.

*

You know, I don't think I can quite believe in suicide.
Although I suppose it could be the solution to Matt's
disappearance. After all, I've just presumed that Matt was
OK with the changes that were going on in his life.
Perhaps he wasn't? Perhaps the desire for something new,
but the inability to work out what, was difficult for him to
cope with. How long had it been going on? Perhaps for
some time. Matt was a very private person, it seems, when
it came to his emotions, and we really can't be at all sure
about his state of mind. He could have been more
confused, disappointed and even more depressed than
anyone knew.

Admittedly Matt had only just put a deposit and a
month rent on the new flat and moved in, which everyone
seemed to feel represented a positive forward move and
therefore counted against the theory of suicide. However,
suicides are often committed at times that seem
inconsistent with other behaviour and ongoing plans, so I
don't think this can be considered against the suicide
theory. Suicide can, I suppose, be planned for, or it can
happen on the spur of the moment.

At the pool that day Matt did not contribute to the
conversation between Paul and RT. He was completely

silent. It was initially reported they thought he was just relaxed and laid-back, busy sun-tanning and not interested in chit-chat, but after RT's 'confession' on the *Sliver* night, I knew a little more of what was going through Matt's head at this time just before he got up, picked up his goggles and went to swim his laps. He was depressed. Confused. Not quite right. RT was scared he might 'do something stupid'.

OK, let's say that Matt decided to leave the pool and commit suicide. So he walks out, wearing his togs and his thongs and his goggles, and then what? Where? He's been driven to the pool by RT and his car is still at Hawthorn so there's no way for him to make a discrete exit from the vicinity of the pool. There's also no way that one of his friends or family would have conspired with him to commit suicide. It's just not feasible. So that's where we come up against a wall, with Matt standing outside the pool, in togs and thongs, carrying his goggles. That's where the whole theory goes haywire. Even if I can accept that he was of the right mindset to commit suicide that day, which I might be able to accept, just, it seems impossible that he could have left the pool to do so.

Unless of course he didn't leave dressed like that. Perhaps he nicked someone else's clothes. I mean, he could have. Perhaps he felt unable to face RT and Paul and go and collect his own clothes. Perhaps he wanted to get out there and do what he had decided upon, without interruption from others. Perhaps he knew that his friends would instinctively notice something was wrong with him and try to stop him. So instead of going back to RT and Paul he could have got out of the pool, gone directly into the changerooms and found there someone's towel, even someone else's clothes, hanging on a peg. I knew from my own visits to the pool that there are always a few people who ignored the signs suggesting that items should not be left unattended. There were always a few towels and clothes on pegs. On a busy day, as it was on the day of Matt's disappearance, it would of course be difficult to find the changerooms empty, but of course he wouldn't have to, he would just have to use the towel and then change into the clothes as if they were his own. Unless the actual owner walked in no one would think anything of it.

So now we have Matt, standing outside the Prahran pool dressed less conspicuously in clothing stolen from the changeroom. Perhaps a pair of knee-length shorts and a teeshirt. Perhaps even a baseball cap? And of course he had his own thongs. His goggles? As they were not found at the pool he must also have had those with him, possibly shoved in his pocket.

And this is where it's interesting to remember some of the sightings of Matt that were reported just after he disappeared. Admittedly there were dozens of them and they can't all be accurate, but I remember there was one person who said they saw someone who looked like the missing swimmer on the Malvern Road tram and a number of people who said they saw a male of around the right age on the beach at St Kilda wearing green and white striped swimwear.

Could that be how he did it? Could that be where he went? First, a short walk from the pool to the Malvern Road tram, down to St Kilda Road and from there on to the St Kilda Beach tram. He did not have his wallet with him of course, and presumably therefore no money to buy a tram ticket, but Melbourne's trams are automated these days and it is possible to travel without a ticket. And when he got there, to a beach full of people, what did he do? Did he simply take off his clothes, those stolen clothes, fold them and leave them on the beach, then just walk into the water of Port Philip Bay? Did he swim out and keep on swimming until there were no other people and no one to see him, right out into the middle of the Bay, where he did a dive down down down towards the bottom and never came back up?

But surely you couldn't just swim out into the Bay and drown yourself without being seen? Surely not. Not on one of the hottest days of summer with hundreds of people at the beach and in the water and jet-skiing and boats everywhere. And surely his body would have been found by now. But no, perhaps not. After all, Prime Minister Harold Holt had disappeared in the surf and his body had never been found. But that was in the open sea, not the Bay.

Admittedly, there had been no reports of any clothing stolen from the Prahran pool on the day Matt had disappeared, and likewise no reports of neatly folded clothes found at St Kilda beach, but perhaps these things were discovered but not reported, not connected to the missing swimmer.

But you know what, the biggest point against the theories of both suicide and voluntary disappearance is the fact that Matt disappeared from the pool in the middle of his laps, with a couple of friends poolside and who knows how many people looking on. If Matt was considering either suicide or voluntarily disappearing, surely he wouldn't choose such a dramatic and difficult place to disappear from. What did this achieve? How would this help him? It couldn't do anything but make it more difficult, more obvious, more suspicious. The only conclusion to come to is that Matt himself would never have chosen to disappear from the pool for any reason, and so I'm left feeling that Matt's frame of mind at the time of his disappearance is therefore irrelevant, that the only explanation has to be that someone else was responsible all along.

But who? Who would abduct Matt from the Prahran pool? Who could have? The obvious suspect, at least in the opinion of the public for a while there, was Kevin. Remember the headline, MISSING SWIMMER: PARTNER FLEES? After the revelation that he was in severe financial difficulty due to the split with Matt, after the anonymous phone call that said the missing swimmer was buried 'in a Prahran backyard' he had been suspect number one there for a while.

Even though the backyard of their Prahran terrace had been dug up and revealed nothing, could Kevin still have killed Matt? Firstly, would he really want to? I guess he could have. Even if the financial reason wasn't enough, he could also have been upset about the failure of his relationship with Matt. But enough to kill him? Somehow, remembering Kevin, so tidy and tight-lipped, clean-shaven and with those rimless glasses, I just can't picture it.

What about Noah. He's as loopy as the day is long. He had an unnatural obsession with Matt, and though this seemed to have been totally innocent, could there have been more to it? Noah, by his own confession, had followed Matt, had stolen items from his washing line, had

138

fantasised about him. Could he have done more? I can, at less of a pinch, believe it of Noah.

Kevin, remember, was 'working from home' that day, not that this means anything other than he was only a few streets away from the Prahran pool and on hand. Noah, though, was at work that day and so, it seems, could not have been directly involved in the disappearance.

Of course it didn't have to be one of those two. It could have been a total stranger, someone Matt had never seen before in his life. The key here, I suppose, is how this stranger, whoever they might have been, could have managed to get him outside the pool, without him going back for his belongings or to tell Paul and RT where he was going, and presumably then into a car and away from the scene.

The last part could be done relatively easily. Think about Ted Bundy and how he lured his victims into his car, either with a fake cast on his arm or leg, struggling with an armful of books, or by pretending to need their help loading and unloading a kayak or a bicycle or something. I can perhaps imagine this working if Matt found someone struggling in one of these ways on the street, or in a car park. He was a strong and fit young man, certainly, and it doesn't seem at first likely that he could be overwhelmed or stuffed into someone's car against his will, but I suppose anyone can be taken by surprise. Hit on the head. Maybe chloroform or something? The thing is, he wasn't in the street or a car park, near a convenient vehicle, he was inside the grounds of the Prahran pool. Surely nothing along these lines could have been done to him anywhere inside the pool grounds, or any of the pool buildings. It's ridiculous to think that Matt could have left the pool anything other than conscious and walking under his own steam. So this stranger, if they existed, must have lured Matt outside first before any move was made. But how?

What if it wasn't a stranger as such? What if it was someone Matt knew? Perhaps not someone he knew well, but a face he knew, a fellow regular lap-swimmer.

This instantly makes me think of that blond man Matt was seen talking to in the shallow end of the pool that day. A woman saw them and reported it, and that lifeguard also saw them and even heard a little of their conversation, even if he couldn't remember the exact words. They seemed, the lifeguard had said, to be acquaintances but not friends. This blond man has never been identified, has never come forward, despite frequent appeals in the press. Isn't that, in itself, suspicious?

Actually, one thing I've just remembered. The lifeguard could not identify the blond guy from the pool database, and in fact did not even recognise him as having been to the Prahran pool before, so therefore it's unlikely that Matt knew this man from lap-swimming. So where did he know him from, then? Work? Mutual friends? Surely someone from one of those groups would have come forward or been identified by now, if so.

Perhaps, though, the blond man was someone Matt knew from the sex-on-premises venue? If so, it makes me wonder whether the lure used to get Matt out of the pool grounds could have been sexual.

Perhaps the blond said that he lived close by. Or maybe that his car, with tinted windows and plenty of room in the back seat, was parked down a discrete side street nearby. Perhaps he suggested to Matt they go out to his car straight away, right then. Emphasising that he had to go soon. That there wasn't much time. Just a quickie. Maybe just a quick head-job? No, don't tell your friends. They won't miss us. You'll be back before you know it.

Would Matt do that? Leave the pool and his belongings and his friends to have a quickie with a blond? I guess he'd have to be quite horny and excited to agree to it. But maybe he was. Maybe he was the sort of person for whom semi-public sexual activity and the possibility of getting caught was exciting. Maybe he enjoyed having sex on the beach, or in the middle of an oval in the dead of night, or in the back seat of a car. Not that he would have needed to have a fetish for sex in cars to agree to it. I don't have that particular fetish, but quite frankly back in the days when RT was a fantasy rather than a reality in my life, if he'd come up to me at the shallow end of the pool and said 'how 'bout it?' I wouldn't have declined. In fact I would have followed him directly out to his car. Towel? Huh? What towel? In any case, the point is that it is a possibility that Matt left the pool with the blond man willingly, perhaps but I suppose not necessarily for sexual reasons. Is it feasible? Certainly no one reported seeing them leave together, but that doesn't mean it didn't happen. Someone may have noticed them, but if Matt walked willingly beside the blond into the foyer and outside, they would have attracted no special attention and quite possibly no one would have noticed them. By that time as well, the staff member on the front desk was dealing with a large number of people and admitted she did not necessarily take notice of people leaving, or going out and back in for a smoke break or whatever. Ironically the fact the crowd increased so much later that afternoon possibly contributed to the fact that Matt was not seen leaving the pool. For he certainly must have done. Either by himself or with someone else.

At this stage, out the front of the pool, both Matt and the blond would still be in only their togs. Or maybe not. The blond may have had a bag with him, in fact probably did if he was swimming, and may even have given Matt a pair of shorts or a teeshirt to wear or something.

Presumably the blond man had a car parked nearby. Perhaps it was parked down a side street. Perhaps the windows were tinted. And when they got to the car, what happened then? Did they get in the back together? Did they have some kind of sex? Or do we just presume that as soon as the doors were closed something, whatever it might be, was done to Matt? Whether he was hit on the back of the head with a spanner or stabbed or had his throat cut. Something.

And from there? Well, once Matt is out of the pool and dead in the back of a car, there are all sorts of permutations. The ocean. A basement. A backyard. An abandoned warehouse in Kensington. Or even that old chestnut, the shallow grave in bushland. Although I don't see why it's always got to be shallow. Maybe the blond had time to dig it really deep.

9

Elle McPherson had been in the news some time earlier that week, in trouble for saying she 'tans safely'. The Cancer Council johnnies on hearing this threw up their lab-coat-clad arms and said there was no such thing as safe tanning and that tanned skin was in fact skin 'in trauma' trying to protect itself against cancer. After that I wasn't able to look at my nice golden glow in quite the same way. The day after the *Sliver* night I smothered myself in 30+, wore an old baseball cap and sat in the shade up the top of the stands at the pool all afternoon reading. The next day I went to a doctor at a local clinic and asked him to check out my various little spots and freckles. The doctor tut-tutted a bit at my tan, but I told him how I wear 30+, a hat and sit in the shade, which is kind of like saying you're a non-smoker when you're only 24 hours into a cold-turkey effort—it's not a lie, but it's hardly the whole truth and nothing but. He didn't seem to believe me anyhow, and fingered my back and my tummy and said that most of what I called moles, were in fact what was known as 'senile warts'. Quite frankly I would prefer my skin be in trauma than senile. He also found one or two blemishes that he 'wasn't sure about' and so after a jab of something he lopped them off with a little scalpel and said he'd send them for tests. One was just under my left nipple, the other low down on my right side. My legs were free of both suspicious moles and senile warts. My ass was lily white and pure, in one respect at least. In fact I had a whole speedo-worth of pearly white skin as pure as the day is long. However, this didn't count and old Doc Smiley told me to lay off the tanning and keep safe.

But quite frankly safety was beginning to shit me. Lung cancer from the smokes, liver failure from the booze, skin cancer from the tanning, heart attack from the battered foods and of course all the dangers of anonymous sex no matter how careful you were to catch up all your drips and spurts and leakages, tie a little knot in them and throw them in the bin. It seemed everything we did was killing us, bit by horrible bit. It just made me want to yawn. Maybe it was kind of morbid to say, but wasn't that what life in fact was—death, bit by lovely, yummy, tasty, exciting, dangerous, bit?

One time when me and Leo were stoned we were talking about this exact thing and decided it'd be a great idea if you lived your life backwards through these little bits of death. This was down the coast from Barcelona somewhere at one of the Costas, you know, Costa Dorada, Costa Blanca, Costa Brava, Costa something else. We were staying in this place which was a total hovel, but with the most glorious view across the top of a terrace of big pinky-red flowers, which I think are called poinsettias, to a blue ocean. It was magic. We set ourselves up at the window ledge with a couple of chairs and took turns to go downstairs to the bar to get takeaway jugs of sangria. We got drunk and stoned and decided it would be kind of nice if everything was reversed and we were born at the moment of what is now our death, and we lived our lives aging backwards, so that we became younger and stronger and more beautiful and all our indiscretions and mistakes and the dangerous things we did day by day were steadily erased rather than compacted and we would wake up every morning and look in the mirror to see one more line is erased and our skin is a bit tighter on our bones, our hairline has crept forward another hair or two, our teeth are whiter and stronger, our eyes a little clearer and we feel increasingly hornier than we ever remember feeling before. Stronger erections more often. Soupier jizz. Quicker recovery time. All the millions of little degenerations that happened day by day replaced with daily regeneration. It seemed like a wonderful sort of Dorian Gray existence, without the portrait in the attic, until of course we spun the whole silly thing out to its inevitable bleak conclusion which saw us revert further backwards through a pimply and uncertain adolescence until we shrank into infancy and dementia and ended up tracking down our mothers in order to crawl up her cunt and disappear forever.

The horror of our sick imagination could only be erased by a swim and an evening of seafood and more sangria, but for a long time afterwards we would remember that stoned idea partly with a shiver and partly with a snigger at how much we'd freaked each other out. I remember it now, now that I can start thinking about that time again at all, kind of fondly, in that way that even the most horrible of events, successfully survived, somehow lose their teeth.

In Spain rules were made to be broken: scooters swept around corners like flocks of birds, dodging pedestrians; passengers smoked on trains directly under no smoking signs; a taxi driver once swore at me for putting on my seatbelt, as if it was an insult. People stay out all night, they drink and smoke and take drugs, sing loudly and tunelessly and are incredibly sexual. Everything seemed edgier and a little bit dangerous. Even the silhouettes of children on Spanish 'Beware of Children' road signs look like rule breakers, a million miles away from similar silhouettes on Australian road signs. In Spain the kids look completely crazy, with legs and arms and plaits flailing. It seems entirely likely they *will* run directly onto the road from between two parked cars at any given moment without looking. But in Australia, the silhouettes are of these freakishly staid-looking midget-adults from the 50s, who look more likely to read Enid Blyton than run into the traffic. When I first returned to Australia from Spain, or to be more specific when I finally got out of bed a week and a half after returning to Australia from Spain, the message of these silhouettes seemed clear as a bell to me. Melbourne was sluggishly slow and stifling, yawningly safe—and over-regulated. Everyone was paying attention to all the rules, obsessive about safety in a creche-like environment in which there was no danger. It made me want to speed in the streets and smoke on the train, shout for no reason and grab the ass of hot men in the street.

But that day after I'd got my two moles cut off, I saw that there was in fact danger here and what's more that I'd been silently surrounded by it ever since I returned. The danger here lay in the nature of the country itself, all year round, but especially in summer, and especially in the dead-time where one year becomes the next. Clear hot days, calm and serene on the surface but dangerous underneath. With the fuss and purpose of everyday life on hold for a couple of weeks, stuffed from Christmas lunch, dizzy from one too many drinks on New Year's Eve, moving slower in the heat, we are dazed, hung-over and vulnerable at a time when our country is more vivid, more alive, and more dangerous than ever. A country under a fierce sun where skin goes into trauma, where bushfires rage and cast a pall of oppressive smoke over whole states, where drought conditions stretch over so many years that winter, real proper winter with water lying around beside the roads and dams full and overflowing, is a childhood memory only, where snakes come out in dry paddocks or slither across suburban back yards in search of water, where jelly fish float in the surf and leave a string of stings across a swimmer's stomach, where in the news guaranteed every summer there will be at least one surfer taken by a shark, where we tally our Holiday Road Toll and compare it to the same time the previous year. And all the while the majority of us are just snoozing on the couch.

It is also a country where a prime minister was once lost in the surf and never found, where three children were once taken from a beach and never found, and where more recently a swimmer disappeared without a trace from a local swimming pool. It's hard to believe that the Australian summer didn't just gobble them all up and spit out the pips.

Had Australian summers always been this nasty? This dangerous? Were they getting worse? Or was it just me and the remnants of my black mood? And whatever the answer, did our precautions make any difference? Were we saving ourselves from anything, or were we partaking of death and disappearance little bit by little bit just as we always had been? In any case, I got the biopsy results back and all was good. My skin was in trauma, my warts were senile, but my moles were benign.

*

I woke up in the middle of the night one night around that time with a lazy hard-on, like you do, and the sensation of Red Trunks asleep behind me. I rolled over to see if he was in the mood for a half-asleep fool around, but forgot that RT wasn't there.

This made me think about Noah. In the transcript he said he used to leave the window open when he went to bed, because he 'knew' Matt Gray would come to him in the middle of the night, this man who he'd never actually met. And that he would be gone again by morning. And I imagined this Noah, how he would wake in the middle of the night (like I just had) in a warm bed, alone (as I was) with the sheets untucked and the dreamy remembered feeling of being touched, of being held, and instead of realising that it was just his imagination (as I did), Noah 'knew' it was him, Matt, and that he had been there, had definitely been there, moments before, and had just crept away through the window.

I couldn't stop thinking about it, how sad it was, and how interesting that this Noah chump was convinced he was having a relationship with a man he had never met and didn't know, and that I was just as convinced I wasn't really having a relationship with the man I was apparently having one with.

*

The next afternoon I was back at the pool. It was one of the most perfect days, only just warm enough, an ever so slight breeze I could see in the hairs on my arm and in the flutter of the flags across each end of the pool but couldn't feel. It must have been the exact temperature of my blood. Hardly anyone was there, which kind of released me from the need to perv, which was actually a relief. No Bastey Boy. No Mrs Crumpet. No Red Trunks.

The water was so crisp and clear and invigorating that when I jumped in and did a walking dive into my first lap, I found an instant limber rhythm which allowed me to go straight through twenty freestyle without a rest. I had become quite strong at freestyle over the summer, so my back was strong and my shoulders and arms sinewy with muscle, but freestyle was all I ever did—if I tried backstroke or kick-boarding, or even heaven forbid butterfly, I'd be buggered after one lap. It was kind of strange that I could be relatively fit at one exercise and still couldn't climb stairs without puffing. But that day those twenty laps felt wonderful and strangely easy. And when I stopped at the deep end and trod water for a few minutes rest, with my arms going back and forward and my legs twisting under me, I felt adrenalin flood through my body like an injection of wellbeing and I suddenly felt sure that God was in his heaven and all was right with the world. I took a deep breath and let myself slip under the water, twisting from side to side with my eyes closed, twisting my legs, my shoulders, my head from side to side. Then I floated up to the surface, snorted the last of my breath out through my nose, took another and arched backwards. My skin felt all over bubbles, like one of those champagne ads at the tram stops, and I floated into a blind backwards somersault.

Seconds later I was clinging to the edge of the pool. My heart was beating like crazy. My arms and legs had pins and needles, like the blood was draining from them to my heart. I floundered out of the pool and back to my towel, trying to control my breathing.

So what was that all about?

Disoriented under the water I had panicked slightly, sure, but after opening my eyes and relaxing I naturally righted and floated up to the surface. No, there was something else that had freaked me out just then, and I knew what it was. I had felt suddenly and irrationally scared that I was going to disappear too.

*

Just like Kevin, I fled. Fled the pool and the panic attack. On the way home I got some vodka and even had a few sneaky sips on the tram. There was no mini-bar at Sharon's Place, unlike a certain hotel in Barcelona I might mention, so I had to buy my own. But Stoli is Stoli the world over, which is a comforting thought I guess.

Back at Sharon's Place some odd vodkas later in the afternoon, it was still quite hot and the air conditioning didn't appear to be working. I was sitting on the kitchen floor in my underwear, with my legs splayed and my thighs cooling on the tiles, like some shaggy pet trying to keep cool. A vodka on ice sat beside me and a whole lot of newspapers were scattered over the floor in front of me.

What the fuck was I doing now? Well, I was doing a bit of messy researching, looking through all the old newspapers I could find and giving myself a recap on the whole missing swimmer case. I'd kept all my old newspapers in a cupboard, meaning to put them out in the recycling, but I never got around to it. So, that afternoon when I inadvertently opened the cupboard where they were and they tipped forward and threatened to fall out at my feet, I virtuously (and a little drunkenly) decided to do the recycling right then and there. I pulled them all out onto the floor, noticed on one an old headline about the missing swimmer and so sat on the floor to read it. It was an early article. One I'd forgotten. After that I just went on doing it. Dragging them all out and going through them, finding the articles about the missing swimmer, flicking through, scanning, rereading

The vodka was making me fixated, helping me become blinkered on this little distraction. But even as a distraction it wasn't quite working. I was only too well aware of something hovering there in the background. It had been there ever since the panic attack at the pool. Longer.

On the newspaper on top of the pile was the picture of Matt with Gil's disembodied arm in the background, hovering behind him, touching him on the small of the back. I felt, suddenly, stupidly jealous of that touch, which had been photographed and printed and circulated throughout all of Melbourne. Everyone knew Gil as Matt's friend. No one knew him as Red Trunks. No one knew he had been putting his arm at my back for the last few weeks. There was no photo of that, was there?

Red Trunks himself hadn't been to Sharon's Place since the *Sliver* DVD blow-up, an absence which could not be blamed on Sharon Stone alone and which I didn't want to think about. Not that the newspapers were successful in distracting me from this either. In fact hadn't RT been little more than a distraction himself? Well, no, that was perhaps unfair, he was a lot more than that. Or, actually, was he? I didn't quite know what he was. I was reminded of a report of mine from my final year at primary school which said I 'promised much but delivered little'. What a crappy thing to write on a school report.

I had a mouthful of vodka, not a sip a mouthful, but found it was mostly ice. Another one gone. I needed a refill, so got up, a bit unsteady perhaps, and got it.

When I turned back I got a jolt and felt myself blush at all those newspapers all over the floor open to articles about the missing swimmer.

In a rush I remembered a newspaper story I'd read way back, when? Maybe in the mid 80s some time? It told how two or three suitcases of newspaper clippings on the missing Beaumont children were found by a council worker in an Adelaide rubbish dump. Many of the articles had comments written on them in red pen. Things like 'not in sand hills, in sewage drain' or 'she used to comb my hair,' written over the image of one of the Beaumont girls. And lots of other things that suggested whoever had clipped out these articles and written on them knew the Beaumont family and had some knowledge of what had happened to the children.

From memory it all blew over in only 24 hours, I think. It turned out that an eccentric old woman who had recently died had spent twenty years collecting newspaper reports about the Beaumonts, but had nothing whatever to do with the case. After the old woman had died, the family had dumped the suitcases at the rubbish tip.

It was an odd little story. And let's face it, the media has finally started eating itself when a newspaper reports on a collection of newspaper clippings—it all becomes a bit spirally and *Vertigo*-ish, one of those forward-tracking reverse shots, which was just what I didn't need right at that moment.

I plonked down again on the cool tiles and looked at all the newspapers, with my bottom lip, slick with vodka, pouting out like a pissed-off kid.

Is this where I was heading with these newspapers strewn over the kitchen floor? Was I going to get out a red felt marker and start making crazy comments all over them? Would they be found after my death, in some suitcase, or maybe stashed in Mr T's porn hideout under the bottom drawer in his bedroom closet?

Porn. Perhaps that was the answer. Perhaps that was it. Perhaps I should get Mr T's porn out and take my mind off things with a bit of self-abuse? But I couldn't be bothered. It was too hot but I wasn't horny at all.

And when they were found, all these newspaper clippings I had kept and written on, would people read the comments I'd made in red marker, comments like 'I knew him' and 'he's in Apsley' and all that shit, and say I was eccentric just like the old woman in the Beaumont case? Would they tell the police not to take any notice, that I'd never known Matt? And RT, would he talk to the detectives in charge of the case and tell them that I wouldn't leave him alone and kept asking about the missing swimmer, and that he'd found it 'pervy'.

But fuck RT. Fuck him as Red Trunks. Fuck him as Gil. And fuck him as Rusty. Who needed him?

I got up again from the kitchen floor, kicking the newspapers into a rough pile in the corner and went out into the beige lounge room of Sharon's Place. From the lounge room I wandered into the bathroom. I felt like Judy Garland or something, wandering around a hotel room vaguely, chock-full of pills and booze and waiting for them to kick in and maybe not remembering how many I'd had.

In the bathroom I avoided my reflection, put my vodka and ice on the toilet seat and lay face down on the tiles. It was cooler there than in the kitchen, where I'd stirred up the air and warmed the tiles with my hot thighs. It felt nice on that floor, almost chilly on my nipples and the underside of my upper arms.

It was such a big floor, like a luxurious king-sized mattress. Even if I stretched out my arms and legs, as if I was doing a big flat star-jump, I could arrange myself so that I wasn't touching anything. Just floating there on the cool surface. I put my cheek to floor and closed my eyes.

That's where I was the next morning.

That day I decided it was time to call Melanie.

*

My conversation with Melanie started off pretty ridiculously really. There was a lot of, It's me. Me who? I'm here. Here where? sort of conversation. But when we finally worked out the basics, Melanie weighed in with 'What happened to Spain?' as if it might have dropped off the map or something.

Silence from my end. I suppose I just wasn't up to the full box and dice explanation, especially not after an afternoon and evening of sustained, not to mention escalating, panic-attack frenzy and drunkenness. Thankfully Melanie, bless her, never needed to understand a situation to come to her own conclusions and usually weigh in heavily on your side.

'That cunt. I knew he was a cunt the minute I saw him. Didn't I tell you? Didn't I tell you?'

I said I didn't remember her telling me that Leo was a cunt, although I admitted it did sound like the sort of thing she might say.

We arranged to meet later that night in town. There was no way I was going to invite Melanie to come up to Sharon's Place. For a start, I just wasn't up to the whole Mr T conspiracy, and anyway I desperately needed out of Sharon's Place, not to mention the mess of newspapers still on the kitchen floor. We agreed instead to meet up at a favourite old hangout in town.

When I arrived Melanie was wary. She got up when she saw me walk in and watched me cross the room like airport security or something, then she kissed me gingerly on the cheek, her eyes swivelled to mine all the time.

'You're looking great,' she started carefully. 'Tanned and healthy.'

I thanked her. Then, having decided I was not about to explode and splatter little pieces of both of us all over the walls, she relaxed into it.

'So what happened to Spain?' she asked again.

Right back where we started.

'I came back,' I said.

'No shit.'

I had to tell her. There was really no way out of it. And so we got ourselves a couple of martinis and I told her what happened to Spain.

*

When I walked out on Leo I was, of course, emotional, but I also remember feeling completely oblivious to everything outside the particular pain I was feeling, and invincible with it, like I didn't need to watch out for oncoming cars, or be careful about suspicious gangs of youths in the backstreets, or worry about getting lost in a city I didn't know where I couldn't speak the language except for *Hola*, because my heart was breaking and that trumped everything. You get me? I was kind of punchy with it. I trudged darkly towards the closest train station, dragging a black suitcase on wheels behind me which tipped over and banged into my heels every second step. At the station I had to contend with ticket machines I didn't know how to use and currency I hadn't bothered to properly understand. Leo used to take care of everything. But I fumbled through the process and when I made it to central Barcelona, I came up the stairs out of the train station, still dragging that fucking suitcase, into a totally deserted street. Huh? I looked to my left, police. I looked to my right, protesters. Somehow I'd walked directly into the middle of an S11 protest route. I was livid. How had this happened? Why was I the only one who had exited the station here? Was there some sign I hadn't understood? Some announcement on the train? How had this happened? And didn't all these people realise my heart was breaking? Callous fucking Spaniards.

156

This may be kind of amusing in retrospect, and Melanie did indeed give a snort of laughter, but it wasn't particularly fun at the time, especially as it was followed by three very bleak days and nights in a hotel that I couldn't afford, getting consistently pissed, with no way to pay the bill, no flight out of Barcelona and no idea what to do. It was the blackest I've ever felt and although I don't remember thinking about it at the time, I look back now and am aware things could have gone another way.

On the third night I called my Mum back in Australia and told her everything. And I can't tell you how good it was to hear an Australian accent. All she actually said when I told her everything was, 'That's no good, Love.' But there's nothing like an Australian mother of 50s vintage to dampen any tendency towards excess melodramatics. After talking to Mum I got my shit together enough to do a bit of online wangling, got myself a new credit card, paid for the hotel bill (please don't ask—I can't think of the amount without wanting to poo) and purchased a return ticket from Barcelona to Melbourne. In the meantime, my sister had managed to tee up a place for me to housesit.

So that's what happened to Spain. It's still there, but I'm not. Just six weeks after jetting off to join Leo in Spain, expecting it to be for good and forever, my tail was between my legs and I was dragging that suitcase back to Barcelona Airport, where there was some minor mix-up about my ticket. Nothing major, but having by that stage all the fortitude of a souffle, I couldn't cope with the questions and burst into tears. Two gorgeous Spanish girls in their BA uniforms crowded around me, took me to a seat, patted me on the shoulder, gave me tissues and got me a drink of water.

'Is it a family member?' one of them asked. I shook my head no.

'Is it a love affair?' the one on the other side asked. I nodded and sobbed out, 'Yess-ss-s-ss.'

They made little noises of sympathy and understanding and patted my shoulder some more, nodding to each other. One of them ended up seeing me to the gate with my boarding pass and waving me off. I must admit I love the fact that an unhappy love affair was their second guess. I had, perhaps, been a little unfair calling all Spaniards callous.

*

Melanie was pretty good actually. She knew that whatever happened in Spain between me and Leo must have been hard and she could see I was, or at least had been until fairly recently, incredibly raw about it, but she listened to what I was prepared to tell her and didn't ask to hear anything more.

Given that I wasn't going to tell her much about me and Leo and that I couldn't tell her about Mr T, it seemed only fair to dish all the dirt there was about RT, so I did, making a big story out of it. She naturally wanted to know all the details of our sex life, which I gave her. I know, trashy, but I had to pay out on something. Then by natural progression we moved on to the fact that RT was Gil who was best mate of Matt Gray.

'Matt what?' Melanie said. She had no idea who I was talking about. It was, actually, kind of refreshing.

'Matt Gray,' I explained. 'He disappeared from the Prahran pool.'

'With a name like that I'm not surprised. He sounds like a paint sample.'

I didn't tell her that RT hadn't stayed at Sharon's Place, nor called me, for three or four days now. Then again, I suppose I hadn't called him either.

In all there seemed to be a million things I didn't want to tell Melanie, which made me feel like a first class shit. However, a bit later that night, after two martinis each, which isn't totally written off but is definitely edging towards it, I told Melanie about my panic attack at the pool, how I had felt suddenly and irrationally scared of disappearing myself.

Amazingly, Melanie started nodding as soon as I began explaining how I'd felt.

'We all get that eventually,' she said. 'It's just your thirties kicking in.'

We talked it out a bit and came up with the theory that people can disappear, or disconnect a bit in their thirties. Just fritz out and lose reception for a little minute before tuning themselves in again. That in our twenties we go on a journey of self-discovery which is endlessly fascinating to us, finding out who we are and what we want and exploring our sexuality and our spirituality and our soul, and discovering others who are like us and just getting our shit together. But then somehow in your thirties it's no longer so internalised and it starts to be more about what you're going to do with what you've discovered, and you start comparing yourself with what other people are doing, and suddenly it seems like everyone else is doing stuff that you should be doing. Everyone else got the jump on you somehow and they've started families and bought houses and shit, or have brilliant careers, or else they just seem so together, or driven, and know exactly what they want. And all your self-discovery stuff doesn't seem quite so relevant anymore, you know, and you feel a bit left behind and translucent.

Melanie ended up telling me not to worry about the panic attack. She said that I'd work it out. I'd tune back in. She also said dryly that I should thank my lucky stars I wasn't a thirty-seven-year-old single woman.

*

The report finally came through that Matt's dental records did not match the charred corpse from the Kensington warehouse fire. The corpse had, however, still not been positively identified. There were many homeless in Melbourne, and the factory was a squat, regularly and irregularly, for a number of them. It was not the corpse of the missing swimmer, but it wasn't the corpse of anyone else at the moment either. Someone else had gone missing, it seemed, but evidently no one was looking for him.

There were suspicious elements to this death and the fire. Firstly, although the rest of the house raised the alarm and were able to escape before being overcome by either smoke or flame, this man did not. Was he already dead? Or perhaps just unconscious? There had been a heavy drinking session earlier in the day. Secondly, there was evidence that the fire was deliberately lit. There was another story about the missing swimmer in the papers that week. Apparently the backyard of the Prahran terrace had been extensively excavated and there was no sign of any body. Kevin, it emerged, was still living in Queensland and was unavailable for comment.

Also, the blond man that Matt was seen speaking to that day at the pool, despite a number of public appeals, including a last ditch one, had still not come forward and identified himself. I wondered why? Either he was in some way implicated in what happened, or else, and somehow this seemed the most likely answer to me, he was totally innocent and didn't even connect himself with the missing swimmer.

None of these news stories rated anywhere near front page treatment. With no fresh leads, no new revelations, and Noah distinctly quiet after his trash-mag 'confession' that never saw the light of day, it seemed that the story had finally run out of legs.

10

I was looking in my case of clothes for a clean teeshirt and noticed a bulge in the lid of the suitcase. I'd forgotten entirely what I'd put in there. I unzipped the pocket and took out a wad of things. Here were photos from Spain. Mostly photos of Leo and me, our heads close together, the camera held at arms length each time so as to catch both of us in front of various Spanish locations. In one shot, the spires of La Sagrada Familia towered over our grinning heads, in others, Gaudi's tiled chimney pots were reflected in our sunglasses, or a Miro sculpture jutted out behind my ear. It was kind of funny to see various Spanish landmarks reduced to an insignificant, sometimes barely distinguishable background to our grinning heads and blossoming, then disintegrating, little love story. In most I looked blissful, but towards the end I was beginning to look worn and slightly wild-eyed.

There were also some sketches I'd made of a crooked cobbled street in Sitges and a canal bridge in Girona, and other sketches from various other places up and down the coast. There was one of Leo sitting across the table from me in an outdoor restaurant, chewing on a toothpick, a jug of sangria on the table in front of him, a woman behind him wearing a fur coat over her shoulders and smoking a cigarette. I remembered her well, talking, smoking, drinking and picking at her fish with a fork all at once all through the meal. I'd drawn arrows with explanatory notes on all of these pictures, which made them more explanations of a scene rather than a visual representation of it, and this woman had an arrow pointing at her saying, talk smoke drink eat repeat.

Lastly there was a plastic A4 envelope with a little press-stud on the front. Inside, stuck onto two or three pieces of paper and carefully preserved between two more blank pieces of paper, were the Polaroid photos. My gut gave a lurch. I extracted them carefully from the plastic. These photos were from much earlier than the others. These were from the year before Spain, when Leo had come back to Australia to visit me a second time, and we had gone on a road trip. From Melbourne we zigzagged up to Sydney for a week, then further up the east coast and into the middle of Australia. I've always loved road trips and this one was extra special. Leo bought me a present before we started. One of those little plastic cameras for kids that took Polaroid photos the size of stamps and you could peel off the back and stick them on things. As we drove we took various photos, again many of them those two-headed ones taken with arm outstretched in front of various Australian landmarks: the Twelve Apostles down the coast road, a yellow diamond road sign with the silhouette of a kangaroo on it, Sydney Harbour Bridge etc. But some were more obscure, like a sky full of seagulls, or spooky ghostly wind turbines in the middle-distance across a paddock, or a weird view of sky and one of the peaks of the Opera House. Even the fuckups we kept, like the one with Leo's finger over the lens, a big blot across the photo, showing skin tone at the edge and pinky-red towards the middle where the sun shone through his blood.

It was Leo's idea, I think, that we stick these Polaroid photographs across the top of the windscreen one by one as we took them. We did so and as the lines of photographs grew from one to two to three to four, we found ourselves overwhelmed by the project. The Polaroid photos became intrinsically part of the road trip and of us being head-over-heels crazy in love. More actually, they were the point of the road trip. We would think very carefully about the photographs we would take next and how they would fit in with the whole. The moment we lobbed with any of my friends during the road trip, we would instantly take them out to the car to look at the Polaroids, overwhelming them with our excitement about the project and about each other. Leo became obsessed with the ritual of cutting off the end tabs of the Polaroid, peeling the backing off and sticking them on the windscreen. We planned never to take them off but instead take the windscreen out of the car and mount it on the wall exactly as it was. So many plans were made, and indeed in all these earlier photographs we look simply happy to be together and fascinated by each other and our journey and by the very photo-project we were appearing in.

I put the Polaroid photos away between their clean sheets of paper and then into their plastic envelope with the press-stud. It clicked closed with such a clipped, buttoned-up, shitty little sound. I put everything back in the suitcase pocket and re-zipped the lid. It felt like I'd found and read someone else's diary.

The next day I finally got to the point where I thought, Oh god, I'm boring myself to death. It's that point that comes out of the blue when you suddenly and inexplicably get over yourself. You realise you're sick of thinking about yourself and your problems and your mind turns away from yourself. It's not like the problems are gone or solved or anything, but it's like you just can't be bothered with yourself any more, you know you're not going to actually die in the gutter or anything, and you just stop obsessing about yourself. It's like when you bring the washing in off the line and turn the pillowslip right side out again. Things are just different.

I'm not sure what brought it on. It might have been the fact that my sister called and told me that Mr T was coming back in a week, so I had to get out, or meeting up with Melanie again; but really I think it was the Polaroids. Finding them made me remember a time when I was happy, and suddenly it didn't seem so impossible that I might be happy again.

*

It was the last week of summer before Melanie and I went to the pool together for the first time. She wore the cutest little 50s style floral bikini, but turned out to be the kind of pool-goer who doesn't actually get in the water. The pool for her was about poolside activity. She set herself up on a banana lounge up on the Lido Deck and proceeded to do her nails, read a magazine, apply suntan cream, and engage in text-message conversations with her friends. Amid all this activity she also managed to confess that she'd talked with Vernon and a few other friends about me and that between them they'd decided they were worried about me and this whole missing swimmer thing. They were of the opinion that hooking up with Matt Gray's best mate, visiting his parents' place, creeping around his childhood bedroom, not to mention rolling around on the floor in newspaper stories about him, which I guess they didn't know about, was just plain obsessed.

I said that perhaps she had a point.

'Why are you doing it?' she asked.

'I don't know,' I sighed.

'I do,' she said with a knowing little look at me, carefully working on her thumbnail with an emery board. 'Because it gives you something to think about other than Spain.'

'That's what all this is about,' she said, and she waved her emery board around the pool to take in everything, the pool itself, but more than that, the routine of the laps which never end, tanning until you're too hot to think, thinking all the time about the missing swimmer, even the nature of my relationship with Red Trunks, sex as sugar pill. That emery board picked out every trick in the book I was using to delay getting on with things, and suddenly I felt like a fool. I was silent. She was, of course, right. It was on the surface all innocent, but it wasn't really, it was all an excuse.

'What happened?' Melanie forgot about her thumbnail and eyed me steadily. 'Tell me. What did he do to you?'

There was nowhere to go. There was no more routine to hide behind. And so I told her. I told her the truth. I told her what he'd done to me, that is, nothing. Leo had done nothing to me. Not a thing. He was all along the most considerate, beautiful, kind, lovely man. I, on the other hand, behaved like a complete fucking asshole most of the time we were together in Spain.

'You did?' Melanie asked.

I did. I was. I had been. And I told Melanie then, right there on the Lido Deck. I told her exactly how I'd been an asshole. How I fucked it all up. I told her everything. And as I told her, as I talked, it all came out of me. Not just the words, but the horrible awful dark feeling that I had been swallowing down ever since I got back. That little ulcer in my gut that made me re-taste whatever I'd last eaten every half hour, on the half hour, with uncomfortable little acidic burps.

I'm not going to write it all down now, because I guess you know it all. When I say you, I mean you, Leo. I guess you know it all because you were there for it. You lived through it. And it's nobody's business but yours and mine. And Melanie's, but she doesn't count. Well, obviously she does, but … never mind.

*

It's about a year and a half on now. I moved out of Sharon's Place and found myself another place to live. Melanie helped me to get some work. I'm back on track. I didn't see RT beyond the end of March, and we don't really contact each other any longer.

I don't think about the missing swimmer much anymore. Neither do the public it seems. After that first two months or so, that summer, there were very few new facts reported. Kevin left Melbourne for good. Noah returned to anonymity and hasn't been heard from since. Apart from that, the corpse burnt in that fire wearing white thongs of the same admittedly very common brand as Matt's remains unidentified, the anonymous caller remains unidentified, and the blond at the pool also remains unidentified. And Matt remains missing. Every now and then there is a story in the paper about him, someone who claims to have seen him, or even claims to be him, but nothing ever comes of it. And as more months go by without any confirmed sightings or new clues, the more we all know there will never be a solution, that Matt Gray will never be found and the mystery of his disappearance will never be solved. But as long as his disappearance remains unsolved, as long as it remains a mystery, he won't be forgotten. The longer we know nothing, the more we will remember.

Personally, looking back from a little distance at that summer, at the missing swimmer and RT and the pool and everything, I feel more and more that I know, deep down, exactly what happened to Matt. I know I only met him once and I never really knew him. But even those people who did know Matt—his family, his best friend Gil, his partner Kevin—admitted they no longer felt they knew him at all. Noah claimed to know him and it turned out he'd never even met him. Matt was a man who had withdrawn, become more distant, less knowable, less real. There were many small reasons for this, I suppose, but no one could say exactly what was wrong, why or when it started, no one could pinpoint an action or a moment, and I think perhaps that's the key to his disappearance. Like dawn and dusk, we can never pinpoint the exact moment that day becomes night or dark becomes light. There isn't a second, a beat, a giant light-switch. It's gradual and creeping and can't be spotted or stopped. It's only when we look up from our book, or out the window as we do the dishes, without having taken any notice of the changing light, that we can say, yes, it is now no longer dusk, it is definitely dark. Maybe it's the same with the difference between being there and not being there. Perhaps Matt started disappearing a long time before the day he actually did. Perhaps he had been disappearing, fading out, for many months, even years. And possibly, just maybe, that day, while doing those never-ending laps, maybe that was only the moment that others around him looked up and noticed, definitely and absolutely, that he was no longer there.